A NEW NOTE

The third book in
the NOTED! series

Kathy J. Jacobson

Kathy J. Jacobson

LITTLE CREEK PRESS®
AND BOOK DESIGN

Mineral Point, Wisconsin USA

Dedication

For "Rick"

Chapter One

Jillian gazed out the breakfast nook window, daydreaming. She never tired of the view of the pool, the orange trees and roses and other blooms. There was always something flowering in the backyard, no matter the date on the calendar. Her eyes moved to the guest house, remembering her special year in residence in said abode, then they jumped to just beyond the cottage where a huge new solar collector had been constructed. Somehow a landscape artist had done a remarkable job of almost completely hiding it from view from the main house while still keeping it functional.

She wondered how it was possible that she and John had already been married for six months. It had been one incredible half year. Auditioning just days after the wedding ceremony, John had returned to acting after a two-year hiatus. Since then, he had done a half dozen projects, all getting outstanding reviews. His agent's phone had been ringing off the hook ever since the premiere of John's first movie project in years, and his subsequent reviews for his role as Mack.

Somehow, between a play, a guest star role on a popular television show, and the start of the filming of the movie, John and Jillian had found a month to take a honeymoon. The trip had included the precious gift of time spent with family and special friends who were like family. Their first stop had been in Chicago, to visit John's nephew, Tommy, his wife, Maria, and their two children. They had toured the future home of Maria's Italian bakery and deli, and served as taste-testers for her special family recipes.

They had watched Tommy and Maria's son, John Anthony, play baseball and later celebrate his high school graduation, and their daughter, Alison, perform an impressive solo on the violin with her orchestra.

From there, they took off for a romantic trip to Italy, which culminated with meeting more of John's family for the very first time. Not only had meeting them been special, but John had received a photograph of his parents and brother that showed a side of his father he had never known. Best of all, his second cousin, Pietro, had given John the gold cross necklace that had belonged to John's mother. His mother had never taken it off, and John had assumed it had gone with her to her grave. Upon its return, John had asked Jillian to wear it, and she wore it daily, just like its original owner.

Their next stop was the continent of Africa, where Jillian introduced John to her loved ones in Tanzania. Jillian and her daughter, Marty, always said that they left part of their hearts in that place, having lived there for eight years while Jillian worked on a mission assignment as a nurse. Jillian had introduced John to her close friend, Loi, and his family, and so many other wonderful people. She found that time had not erased their special bonds, and was especially pleased that Loi had declared that Jillian had found a "good man" in John—not that she had any doubt about that. It made her happy that her friends found him to be as special as she did.

Their final stop had been in Senegal to see Marty in her current African home, Dakar. She was an intern in a hospital and research

Kathy J. Jacobson

facility, part of her program as a medical student at Harvard. Marty had surprised Jillian by introducing her to her special friend, Michael, who was a medical student at Stanford University. They made a wonderful pair, but Marty had concerns about a relationship that would soon have three thousand miles between them when they returned to the States just before Christmas.

Since returning to Los Angeles from their honeymoon, John and Jillian had made some conscious decisions to make life better for others, both near and far. One such decision was to open a non-profit acting workshop, which they hoped would expand to include other types of classes in the future. It had recently been approved at a city council meeting. They had found the perfect building, and the workshop was in the process of becoming a reality, thanks to many friends who were generously donating their gifts of expertise and their enthusiasm along with them.

John and Jillian had also invited their household helper, Esperanza, to move into the cottage behind the house, the one Jillian had occupied when she worked for John in the same capacity. Esperanza would live in the cottage rent-free, while she went to school at night and worked at their home and another home, cleaning on weekdays. Once she got her degree and found a job in her field of study, Esperanza would move out. They hoped to continue the same arrangement for other helpers in the future.

Another project had been the placing of rain barrels at the back of the house, which now watered their many rose bushes and other plants. In addition to the free-standing unit which stood beyond the cottage, solar panels had been installed on the rooftop of the home. The entire property's electricity, including the heating of the pool in the cooler months, was now powered by the California sun.

All of these changes had been by-products of their trip. Their honeymoon had reminded John and Jillian how abundantly blessed they were. The only way they felt they could continue to live on their property was to be better stewards of natural resources, share some of their space, and use some of their individual gifts and material resources for the betterment of others. Their choices could not solve every issue, but they felt that their decisions were definitely steps in the right direction.

The only negative in their first six months of marriage—and it was a significant one—had been the huge scare they received when Marty had been put in isolation in the hospital in Dakar, fearing that she had contracted Ebola. It turned out to be Dengue fever, which while dangerous in itself, was not as deadly as Ebola. Marty was recovering at a slow and steady pace, and was on track to finish her research and be home by Christmas as planned.

So, yes, Jillian thought these first six months of their marriage had been remarkable—that is, until the next six months happened. They would be, as John and Jillian would refer to them in future years, unforgettable.

Chapter Two

It was October 31st when Pete's number flashed across the screen of Jillian's cell phone. Pete was a very dear friend who had married his wife, Kelly, just weeks before Jillian and John took their vows. Now the couple was waiting anxiously to become parents for the first time, expecting twins in late January. Jillian was glad they were living in Southern California rather than her home state of Wisconsin with a due date like that. Driving to hospitals in snow and ice is never a good time.

"How is it going, Pete?" Jillian asked in an upbeat voice.

The usually positive Pete sounded out of sorts. "Jillian, I'm so glad you answered. I'm worried about Kelly," he said.

"What's going on?" Jillian asked, the former nurse in coming out.

"She's had a terrible headache all day and she won't take anything for it. She says she just has a bug—she's a little nauseous, too. She's been in bed all day, and she won't let me call the doctor or go in to the clinic...I don't suppose you could drop over?" he asked.

Jillian was in the middle of writing, but she quickly closed the laptop. "I will be right there," she said, hoping that it was just a "bug" like Kelly had suggested. It was too difficult to know over the phone, and she didn't want to assume it was just a normal pregnancy issue. It wouldn't hurt to take a break and get out of the house—that would be her excuse if Kelly wondered why she was there.

Pete met Jillian at the door. "Thanks, Jillian. You are such a good friend," Pete said, letting out a huge sigh as she stepped through the door. The usually affable, strong, and athletic man had been replaced by a serious, vulnerable and weak impostor.

He gave Jillian a quick hug. "I'm so glad you're here," he said. "She's in our room." He led Jillian down a hallway to the back of the ranch-style home. They passed the nursery, which was nearing completion. There were two cribs and two small dressers set up, and against another wall, a changing table. A small stepladder sat in the middle of the room, as a decorating project was in the works.

Jillian followed Pete through the door and into the darkened room. Pete walked over to Kelly, kissed her forehead, and told her that Jillian had dropped in to visit.

"Jillian, is that you?" Kelly asked.

"Yes, Kelly, I'm right here," she said, moving closer to the bed. "Can you see me?"

"I... it's so dark in here... I wasn't sure it was you," Kelly said, sounding weak and a bit confused.

"Let's open up the blinds, okay, Kelly?" Jillian asked in a gentle tone. She felt like she was back at the hospital in Madison. Pete went over to the window and slowly shed some light on the situation.

Jillian took one look at Kelly and knew it wasn't good. She walked to the bedside and took one of Kelly's very swollen hands, then looked into a puffy face that matched her hands.

"Do you mind if I look at your feet, Kelly?" Kelly didn't answer, but Pete nodded that it was all right, and Jillian slowly pulled back the sheet.

"Kelly, I think the three of us should go for a little ride and have you checked out, just to make sure everything is as it should be," Jillian said calmly.

"Okay," Kelly said in a weary tone.

Fear was etched into Pete's face. Jillian didn't want someone who was that upset behind the wheel of a car.

"Pete, I will drive, if you don't mind. You can snuggle up to your wife on the way," she said with a smile, trying to keep them both calm. Jillian was pretty sure that Kelly had preeclampsia and wished she the equipment to take her blood pressure.

They decided to take Pete and Kelly's vehicle, leaving Jillian's white Land Rover in the driveway. She texted John, who was at a meeting with his agent, Alan, to tell him where she was, and that she wasn't sure when she would be home.

They went to the emergency room, just in case Kelly needed to be admitted to the hospital. It was a good choice.

Kelly's blood pressure was 175 when they arrived, and had risen to 180 after fifteen minutes. Her doctor was reached and came in to consult with the physician at the hospital. They decided that the best course of action was to deliver the babies immediately via a c-section, since Kelly's liver enzymes were also elevated. The doctors wanted to move quickly before the situation became even more dangerous.

The doctors left the room. Pete was beside himself. Kelly was tired, as her severe headache and sky-high blood pressure had drained any energy she had.

"Jillian, how can they come so soon? It's only about 30 weeks," Pete said, starting to panic "They won't make it, will they? They're too little."

Jillian walked over to him and put her hand on his arm. "Pete, the doctors wouldn't suggest this unless it was best for Kelly and the babies," she said. "Babies, especially twins, often don't make their full term. This is a good hospital, with an excellent NICU—neonatal intensive care unit. They will take good care of them."

Pete sat down on a nearby chair, looking slightly unsteady on his feet. Jillian thought he might be feeling lightheaded. "This is all my fault," he said.

"Pete, stop it. There is no way any of this is your fault. Thank goodness you called me, especially since Kelly wouldn't let you call the doctor or take her in earlier. If anything, you saved the day," Jillian said.

Pete put his head into his huge hands and raked his fingers through his thick, dark curls. "What do we do now?"

"Pray," Jillian said, matter-of-factly.

The surgical staff quickly arrived and began prepping Kelly for surgery. Fortunately, she hadn't eaten anything all day. Jillian hugged a reeling Pete before he headed out the door with his wife. She was almost as worried about him as she was about Kelly and the babies.

Jillian sat down in the chair where Pete had been sitting and took out her cell phone to call John. He had texted her back an hour before, but she hadn't had a chance to respond.

"Are they going to be all right?" he asked in a worried tone after Jillian filled him in on the developments.

"I hope so. Every case is a little different. It will be toughest on the boy. It depends on his lung development. And let's hope

Kelly's blood pressure doesn't spike any higher," she said.

"I'm so glad you went over to their house, Jillian, and that you are there with them. Is there anything I can do to help, sweetheart? Should I come over?" he asked.

"I'm just so thankful Pete called. You don't have to come— I know the day you've had, honey. But you could say a prayer for them..." she said, her voice trailing off.

"Definitely," he said. "I love you, Jillian."

"I love you, too, John," she said, wishing he was there beside her. She had almost told him to come to the hospital, but she knew that his day had been very long and busy, and that he had an even longer and busier one the next. She put her cell in her purse and went to find the chapel to pray for this very special new family.

Two hours later, Pete walked into the surgical waiting room. He looked wiped out, but he also looked hopeful.

"Jillian," he said, "I'm a Dad." He threw his arms around her, tears in his eyes.

"The doctor said they should be fine in the long run," Pete continued. "Our little girl is 3 pounds, 3 ounces. Our little guy is 4 pounds, 5 ounces. I guess he takes after me—they said that's big for a twin at his stage of development. Of course, they will be in intensive care for a while, but considering..." He couldn't finish the sentence.

Jillian squeezed his arms. "That is wonderful news, Pete. How is Kelly?"

"She's in recovery. She should be back in the room shortly. Should we go back there?"

"Sure thing," she said. "I'll meet you there, I just want to let John know—we've both been praying for you."

"Tell him it helped," he said seriously, and then headed back to the room.

Jillian hit the contact number for John. He answered, and she heard his voice—on the phone and for real. She looked up and saw her handsome husband walking toward her, smiling, with two adorable stuffed elephants in a clear bag from the gift shop in his hand, one with pink satin lining in its ears, the other with blue.

She hit the "end call" button and practically ran to him. He put out his arms to her, and she fell into them. He held her tight, rubbing her back with his free hand.

"Any word?" he asked after she pulled back from him.

"You just missed Pete. He's going back to the room to wait for Kelly. She should be back soon. It sounds like it went about as well as it could have."

"I'm so glad," he said.

"I'm *so glad* you're here," she replied, hugging him again.

"So am I. I just couldn't stay away. I also thought you might want to go home sometime tonight."

"Yes, that would be nice, since my car's at Pete and Kelly's house."

"We can get it on the way home, or do it another time if you prefer," he said.

"You're the best, John," she told him.

"I have a good teacher," he said.

She squeezed his hand, then they walked toward the room. She looked down at the bag in his free hand. "So, what did you find in the gift shop? I'm surprised it was even open."

"It was just closing as I walked up to the door. Luckily, the volunteer manning the store used to be a big fan of *O.R.* and she let me in—after I promised to give her an autograph. She helped me pick out these little guys," John said, pulling out one of the soft stuffed animals.

"So, was she pretty?" Jillian asked.

"Yes, very attractive. And in really good shape—for someone who just had her 85th birthday."

"Wow, sounds like the conversation got pretty intimate. How do I know you won't decide you prefer someone more mature?"

"I guess you'll just have to trust me," he said as they arrived at Kelly's room.

Kelly had just arrived moments before them, and the nurse and nursing assistant were making sure all of her IV tubing was untangled. Then they showed her the call button for the nurses' station, how to turn on the TV and answer the phone, and gave other basic instructions to her as well as Pete. They pointed to a dry-erase board on the wall, telling them their names and that they would be there until the next morning.

Jillian was certain that Kelly would be asleep very shortly. It had been a very long, very frightening, and extremely exhausting day.

After the staff cleared out, Pete was at Kelly's side. Jillian and John moved closer to the bed as well.

"Jillian!" Kelly said, with as much strength as she could muster.

"Kelly," Jillian replied, and went over to take the hand of her friend. "I'm so glad you are okay."

"Thank God you came over to our house," she said.

"Yes, thank God, and your wonderful husband."

At that, Kelly reached out her other hand to an equally exhausted, but very relieved, Pete.

"They said we can go in to spend time with the babies in the morning. I can't wait until we get to hold them," Kelly said.

"Well, right now, you'd better get some rest so you can give them all of your attention tomorrow," Jillian recommended.

Kelly yawned, as if that was her answer. "I guess you're right," she said, and began to close her eyes.

"You two should go home," Pete suggested.

"You must be starving, Pete," Jillian said. "Do you want to get something to eat with us, or should we get something for you?"

"I don't think I can leave this room," Pete said.

"I didn't think you would. We'll be right back," she replied. "Or John, maybe you should stay with Pete while I run down to the cafeteria. You can show him what you and your girlfriend in the gift shop picked out for the twins."

Pete looked confused for a moment, but then saw John and Jillian smile at each other. Otherwise, Jillian thought, he might have broken John in two.

Early the next morning, John dropped Jillian off at Pete's to get her car. They were going to stop in at the hospital after John met with the foreman of the building renovations for the actor's workshop and she got done with a meeting with her book editor. A book tour was in the works beginning in late November, and they wanted to make sure that everyone knew what they needed to do and where they needed to be.

The tour would begin in the Los Angeles area, which was perfect, as John and Jillian had Drew and Greta's wedding to attend on Thanksgiving Day in Encino. The original plan had been for the Friday or Saturday of that week, but Jillian's editor insisted she not miss being in the bookstores during the biggest shopping day and weekend of the year. Drew and Greta decided that they would change the ceremony to the day of Thanksgiving, and have a turkey and tofu dinner with just the two sets of parents, Drew's sister and her husband, and John and Jillian afterward. Jillian thought Thanksgiving Day was a great day for a wedding—second best only to John's and her Easter Day marriage.

John and Jillian met at the hospital in the early afternoon. Kelly was improving, and the babies were holding their own. Pete and Kelly had announced the names of their children after John and Jillian arrived in the room. August "Gus" Peter was the name given to their son, whom the NICU nurses affectionately referred to as "Bruiser," and Grace Jillian was their daughter's name.

Jillian was at a loss for words when she heard the little girl's name. John had just beamed and squeezed Jillian's hand. Jillian's first inclination was to protest, but then decided that she should keep her resolution to accept compliments when they came her way. This was by far one of the greatest ones she had ever received.

"Don't be so surprised, Jillian," Pete said. "If you hadn't told me to go to San Francisco and ask for forgiveness, absolutely none of this would have happened. And if you hadn't come over yesterday..." Pete swallowed hard, unable to continue.

"Do you want to see them?" Kelly interrupted, coming to her husband's rescue.

"That would be wonderful," Jillian said.

"Pete, take them down to the nursery and sign them in," Kelly directed. "Maybe I can get some rest while you do." As she said this, she looked at Jillian.

Jillian knew that sometimes family members could exhaust their loved ones, just by trying too hard and never letting people be alone and relax.

"Are you sure, Kel?" Pete asked his weary wife.

"Yes, I'm very sure," she replied, and put her head back on the pillow.

Pete took them down the hall, where a nurse signed them in and gave them visitor badges. Jillian hadn't been in a NICU in a long time, and John had never been in one at all. It was interesting to watch his eyes widen as they passed the small incubators holding even tinier bodies. Some of the babies made Gus and Grace look like giants, and some were obviously not as fortunate as they appeared to be.

Gus and Grace were getting oxygen, but were not intubated. They were fed through tiny "g-tubes" at present, but hopefully in a couple of weeks they could begin to use a bottle. Jillian went to each of them, spoke to them, and rubbed their tiny backs.

"Is it okay if I touch them, too?" John asked, looking completely amazed. Jillian had to remember that he had never worked in a hospital, nor had he ever been a father, except to her fully grown daughter. She wasn't sure how much he had been around his nephew, Tommy, when he was an infant. Even if he had spent time with him, these babies were smaller than the typical full-term baby.

"Sure," Jillian said, and stepped aside for John to touch Gus.

"His skin is so soft," John said in a low voice as he lightly stroked the baby, a smile spreading across his face. Gus yawned the tiniest yawn, and John was absolutely fascinated. "Did you see that?" he asked, with a mixture of excitement and awe.

Pete was the typical proud dad, smiling widely and nodding his head. Then John went over to little Grace and touched her. He was even more cautious with the more petite infant girl. He gently put his fingers on her back and moved them slowly and lightly, and softly spoke to her, "Hello, beautiful Grace Jillian." At that, the baby mouth's curled up. It was just a random movement, but it looked like she had just smiled at the compliment.

"You're charming her already, John," Jillian said to her husband.

"I have that effect on females," he replied.

"I know," she said, clasping her arm around his and hugging it.

They all took turns touching and talking to the babies for another half hour. Then they walked back down to the room.

Kelly was sound asleep. Jillian motioned to John and Pete to follow her out into the hall. She knew it was important for Kelly to rest, and she finally convinced Pete to go downstairs with them and get something to eat for dinner. She kept them all downstairs as long as she possibly could, so poor Kelly could have a break from her very devoted, well-meaning husband.

Before John and Jillian left for the night, she told Pete how very important it was that Kelly get some good rest, without any interruptions, each day. She thought that he was finally beginning to relax a bit and hoped that he might be able to let his wife do the same. They each hugged Pete goodbye, and then took the stairs back to the car.

As they walked through the parking ramp, John took Jillian's hand. He was quiet, and Jillian knew that thoughtful look on his face. He was processing all that he had just witnessed.

"That was miraculous," he said, when they got into the car.

"Another kind of new creation," she answered.

John nodded his head in agreement, still deep in wonder as he started the engine to drive home.

With all the excitement surrounding the early arrival of the twins, Jillian almost forgot her video call date with her daughter that week.

"Marty!" Jillian exclaimed, after running into the room to her computer as it indicated Marty was ringing her.

"Hi, Mom, how's it going?" She didn't even wait for a response. She could see some kind of news in her mother's eyes. "Something happened, didn't it? I can see it in your face."

"Kelly had to have a c-section. She had preeclampsia and was on the verge of the next stage, so they took the babies. They are all okay now, but it gave everyone quite a scare." Jillian went on to tell

Marty the entire story, including the names of the babies.

"That's quite an honor, Mom," Marty said.

"I know. It was a real surprise—a nice one," Jillian replied.

"Well, I have a bit of a surprise—a nice one—for you, too," Marty said, a big smile lighting up her face. "After you left last summer, and before I got sick, I applied for a one-semester exchange project with Stanford. It was pretty much last minute, and I think they already had the person they wanted for it in mind when I got my application in. I had completely forgotten about it, especially after the Dengue fever fiasco, but I just heard from them. The person they had chosen just withdrew from the project, and they offered me the opportunity. So, instead of being in Cambridge next semester, I'm going to be in California!"

Jillian could hardly believe it. Her daughter had been a minimum of a thousand miles away from her for the past four years. While it was a long drive up to Stanford, it was nothing like the long distances between them in recent history.

"That's fantastic, Marty! I can't believe you will be that close to us. And now you and Michael won't be three thousand miles away from one another either!"

"Yes, being closer to the people I love—it's the best!" said her daughter, her eyes shining with happiness.

They talked more about the project and the fact that Marty would stay after Christmas until it was time to go north to Stanford. Jillian was so happy she began to cry, and her daughter followed suit. Not only was her girl coming back to the States—she was coming back to *her* state!

Chapter Three

Jillian was preparing for the launch of her book, which was scheduled for the weekend before Thanksgiving. She couldn't believe it was actually happening. There was a lot of chatter on the blog about it, and it was already being promoted by her publishing company at bookstores, online stores, and even in some medical and mental health communities. Jillian was not only excited about the book, but also the promotional tour, which would include stops at bookstores, libraries, and two medical schools.

Jillian was also enthused because she believed she had the subject of her next book. She was going to write about pregnancy complications and losses. The thought entered her mind the day after Gus and Grace made their early appearances. Jillian had blogged about the experience with the twins and had an overwhelming number of responses. So many people wrote about encounters they, or their friends or family members, had had that she could hardly keep up with them. The stories kept pouring in, and their numbers escalated exponentially.

Jillian had already contacted a number of the contributors about sending her more detailed accounts. She also asked whether or not they would consider letting their stories be a part of a book to help parents who had gone through, or who were at risk of going through, similar experiences. Many people were willing to do whatever they could do to be helpful, no matter how their own stories ended. Some of the stories were miraculous. Others were heart-wrenching.

Gus and Grace fell into the miraculous category, and were growing steadily. They were being fed by bottle now, and both John and Jillian had the honor of feeding them on several occasions. Jillian thought that John would have been a wonderful father. Every time she saw him gently holding one of the babies, talking to them, or rocking them in his arms, a twinge of regret would shoot through her. She couldn't help but wish that he was holding *their* baby, but after the last few weeks visiting the NICU, she knew they were making the right choice by not attempting such a feat at this stage of their lives. Instead, they would have to be satisfied with being the parents of one very special twenty-six-year-old, and also godparents to Gus and Grace, as Pete and Kelly had recently honored them with that request as well.

Pete had finished the nursery in their home and had gone back to work. It was difficult for him to be away as the owner and manager of a brand new fitness center. Thank goodness he had hired an excellent assistant manager for the club shortly before the twins' untimely arrival. He stopped at the hospital every morning and after work each day to hold, feed, or diaper the babies, his huge hands fumbling with the tiny bodies and equipment. He was getting more adept each day. The nurses marveled at how minute the twins looked whenever he held them, however, compared to everyone else.

Kelly was able to take some extra time off as family medical leave, although once she was up to it, she began to do some work from her computer, sometimes from the hospital lounge when the babies were sleeping. She wanted to make certain that she would maintain all of her maternity leave once the children came home, so she didn't mind doing the work. If the babies kept progressing the way they were, they were slated to go home a week, possibly two weeks before their actual due date. Pete and Kelly couldn't wait to get them home and establish some kind of normalcy, if one can have a normal life with twins in the house. Still, considering all that had transpired—and all the possible outcomes—they were feeling very blessed.

Jillian was just thinking about what she and John should give their godchildren as baptismal gifts, when her cell phone chimed. Karen's number flashed, and Jillian smiled as she answered the call. Karen and her former workaholic husband, Robert, who as Karen liked to say was now in "recovery," had been traveling over a long weekend, this time on a wine-tasting tour in the Napa Valley.

"Jillian, it's been way too long," Karen said when Jillian answered.

"I agree, Karen. Between my book preparing for its debut and our friends, Pete and Kelly—you met them at our wedding reception—having twins born early, it's been tough to connect. I'm putting together my presentation for the promotional tour, and we're also going to be godparents to the babies. I just haven't gotten around to normal things lately—like calling my good friends!"

"I completely understand. I haven't been any better. Between school and our getaways, it's been pretty crazy," Karen said, then asked more about the twins.

Jillian filled her in with the two-minute version of the saga, and was happy to report such a good prognosis.

"Well, while we're on the subject of children, what do you know about foster parenting?" Karen asked.

"It can be challenging, but it can also be incredibly rewarding, and sometimes life-changing—even life-saving—for the child involved. Why do you ask?"

"There's a boy in my class whose father just went into the hospital, and it doesn't look good," she said. "They can't seem to locate any family members, and the boy doesn't know of any. He's one of my favorite students—so kind, helpful, and smart. I guess when the social worker asked him if he could think of anyone he could live with, he said *me*! I was flabbergasted, but then I felt very honored. I asked Robert about it. He said he's willing to think about it. They want to know in a week, because his temporary foster home time is going to be up soon."

"Wow, it's really nice that the boy feels so strongly about you. Personally, I think you and Robert would be wonderful foster parents," Jillian said.

"Really? You *really* think so?"

"I really think so, Karen. You have a lot of love to give, and you have many other advantages that you both could share with someone who does not," Jillian said.

"I never thought about it that way," she responded. "We completely put the thought of children out of our minds after all the years of trying...it was just too painful to think about them. I think it's part of the reason Robert started working so many hours all those years ago."

"Maybe this is the time for you both to start thinking about it again, and to be a parent to someone. Sometimes things happen in very strange ways—just think about how John and I got together," Jillian said. "After all those years as an unmarried mother, nurse, a person who shied away from relationships after two great disappointments in that area, I move to California, end up working at John's house, and fall in love with him during one very crazy year. Now I can't even imagine my former life anymore."

"That's true, Jillian. Maybe this is meant to be," Karen said, her mind far away. "I'll talk to Robert tonight. I'll let you know what we decide."

"Please do," Jillian replied.

"And Jillian, would you pray for us to make the right decision?" Karen asked. Karen was not a churchgoer, although from time to time she asked Jillian more about it, and this was the second time she had asked her to pray for her. The first time was when she was at the end of her rope with Robert.

"Of course I will, and so will John," Jillian said.

"Thank you," she responded. "The last time it seemed to work."

"It always works, Karen, but not always the way we would like. I prayed long ago that Marty's father would marry me, but he didn't. Now, I can't imagine my life without John. If I had married Marty's father, there would be no John. Sometimes the answer we receive is 'yes,' sometimes 'no,' sometimes 'not yet,' or 'not this one,'" Jillian said.

"I never thought about it that way. I only know..." Karen responded, her voice dropping off.

"I'll look forward to hearing from you," Jillian said. Jillian imagined that there may have been a time when Karen had prayed and prayed for a baby, but it didn't happen. She would pray that God would heal her heart now, just like God had healed hers.

Chapter Four

John came into the kitchen with a stack of scripts in his arms, then dropped them onto the counter. This had become a weekly ritual ever since his movie had premiered.

"I was going to ask you what your plans were after dinner tonight, but I think I have my answer," Jillian said, eyeing the pile of papers.

John sighed. "It's going to be an all evening affair again, I'm afraid," he said as he hugged her. "I'd rather spend it with you," he added, and kissed her forehead.

"I got a lot done today, so I could help you go through them," she said.

"You've been staring at a computer all day, and you want to read scripts all night?" John asked, still holding her.

"As someone once told me, as long as I'm with you, I don't care where we are or what we are doing," she said, looking into his deep brown eyes.

John shook his head and put his fingers gently under her chin. "How did I get so lucky?"

"I was just wondering the same thing," she said, then kissed him.

The script reading session was long and frustrating. John couldn't believe that in all the scripts he had perused over the past month, there wasn't something that stood out. Sometimes the two of them found themselves laughing out loud, trying to imagine John actually playing a particular part, or wondering how something so mediocre could have gotten this far along in the process.

They were planning to have three piles on this night—yes, no, and maybe. John was looking for something thoughtful and well-written. He had always been a stickler when it came to the writing, and had been spoiled after working on *O.R.*, which had had a team of award-winning writers. Writing could make or break a television show or movie, no matter how talented the actors.

Most of the movies were stories with mass appeal, but had little else to offer. At this point in his career, John was looking for something special. He was least interested in the romantic comedies, although Jillian enjoyed reading the parts of his love interests. John mentioned that they had to stop acting them out, however, or they would never get done.

At 2:00 a.m., John let out a weary sigh and put the last script on the "maybe" pile. Unfortunately, they only had two piles at the end of the night—no and maybe.

Nothing really struck either of them as "just right," but new offers were coming in almost every day. Luckily, John didn't have to make a decision on any of the current ones immediately, but he would definitely turn in the "no" pile the next day.

John also planned to find out who the intended directors were for the "maybe" pile. The best script may not reach its potential under the wrong guidance, and a clash of personalities could ruin a project as well.

"Enough," John said, putting his arm around Jillian's shoulders as they sat on the couch. She put her head on his shoulder and closed her eyes.

"There must be something better out there, something meaningful," John said, caressing her arm.

"You mean you really think there's something better out there than *Sad, But True*?" she asked teasingly, referring to a romantic comedy script that had gone quickly into the "no" stack.

"Talk about an appropriate title," he said, rolling his eyes.

"But John, it has such memorable dialogue," she continued. "*I can't remember my phone number. Can I have yours?*"

He surprised her by flipping her onto her back until her head rested in his lap. She found herself looking straight up into his eyes. "*Too late, you already have my number,*" he said, reciting the line, then kissed her sweetly. Afterward, he gently pulled back, his face just inches from hers.

"See, I told you it was good dialogue. It worked, didn't it?" she said in a soft, playful tone.

He just smiled and kissed her again.

The next afternoon John came bounding into the kitchen, a script in his hands.

"I think this is it, Jillian!" he exclaimed. "Will you read some of it and see what you think? Carson Stone is directing it and asked for me—to play the lead male role." He sounded like he didn't quite believe it.

"Wow—Carson Stone. Let's have a look at it. And John, you shouldn't be so surprised. You are an amazing actor, and it's time you accepted that fact," Jillian said, putting her hands on his chest.

"You're only saying that because you're crazy about me," he joked.

"It's true, I *am* crazy about you, but give yourself some credit," she said, then kissed his cheek.

"I'll try," he said, a dreamy look on his face.

"Breakfast nook? Library? Couch?" Jillian asked, suggesting places for the reading.

"We'd better stay away from the couch," he said teasingly.

"Okay, to be safe, let's stay in the kitchen," she said.

"I'm not sure any place is safe with you, but it's the best we can do," he replied, as they both slid into the two wooden benches of the breakfast nook and faced each other.

The story was a suspenseful drama concerning the Alaskan pipeline. It reminded Jillian of *The China Syndrome*, a hit movie made in 1979 about a near nuclear disaster. Like that movie, this one would have a large cast of characters. The leading role John would play would be that of a scientist. Of course, he would have a love interest in the movie, a veteran reporter sent to investigate his claims.

Jillian knew, especially after reading through all the scripts in the past month, that it was inevitable that John would have to kiss other women, and perhaps even more than that. She was working on mentally preparing herself for the situation. This movie would have quite a bit of kissing in it and one bedroom scene between John and the female lead. At least it wasn't very long—but it was there—in "full living color," as her mother used to say.

Jillian wondered if they had anyone in mind yet for the female lead and asked John.

"So, who gets to kiss you?" she asked after they read through a good portion of the script.

"I guess that is still up in the air. Alan said Carson had someone in mind, but he hadn't heard back from her. If that person doesn't do it, they might do auditions. I guess they are trying to assemble a fairly star-studded cast," he said.

"It seems like a great story, John. It's meaningful, suspenseful, and of course, there's a bit of romance for those of us who enjoy that. It seems to have very intelligent dialogue and might help people think a bit more seriously about environmental issues. Scripts like this one, along with a top director, rarely come around," she said.

John nodded his head in agreement. "Exactly my thoughts. I think I should do it, if you are okay with that?"

"John, you don't need my permission," Jillian said. She could see the excitement in his face, and it made her feel good inside.

"I know, but I'd like your blessing," he responded thoughtfully.

"You'll always have that, John. Whatever makes you happy, makes me happy," she said, meaning it.

John took her hands in his, then brought them to his lips and kissed them.

"I sure do love you, Mrs. Romano," he said.

"That's good, because I sure love you, Mr. Romano," she responded. "Now, you'd better call Alan. I would bet he's sitting with the phone in his hand, just waiting for you to call."

Jillian was right about that, as Alan answered on the first ring.

"Tell them to send over the contract, Alan," John said, beaming at Jillian across the breakfast nook table, still holding one of her hands in his free one.

"Ah...sure. I will. Ah..." Alan was stammering on the other end of the phone. It wasn't exactly the reaction John was expecting from this long-time friend and agent.

"Is there a problem, Alan?" John asked, the smile beginning to fade slightly from his face.

"Ah... they heard back from the actor who will play the female lead," he said.

"So, who is the lucky woman?" John asked, trying to tease Jillian and wondering why Alan was acting so peculiar.

He got his answer a moment later. John turned as white as a sheet, and Jillian thought he might pass out. John ended the call, put the phone down on the table, and just stared ahead, looking straight through her. Jillian felt worried for a moment. The possibility of John having another brain tumor was always something that lingered in the back of her mind.

"John," Jillian said in a concerned tone, squeezing his hand. "What's the matter?"

He just said two words, ones that smacked her right in the face and would continue to ring in Jillian's ears the rest of the night and into the next few days.

"Monica Morgan."

Chapter Five

"I'm going to call Alan back and tell him I'm not going to do it," John said after a minute of silence on both their parts. Jillian was almost as stunned as John, and the right words hadn't registered in her brain, so she said nothing.

Finally Jillian spoke. "John, it's such a perfect part for you, and such an important film. I think you should think about it some more. You haven't signed anything yet, so you have until at least tomorrow morning." She heard herself speak, but it was as if she was listening to someone else. She was trying to remain calm and say the right, supportive things that a good spouse should say, even though there was a part of her deep down that was definitely reaching panic mode.

Of all the female actors in the world, what were the chances of this happening? Then again, the two of them had had incredible chemistry in their hit television show, when Monica played Dr. Pamela Prine and John portrayed Dr. Nick Caruso, so of course, Monica was a logical choice. And of course, they had had great chemistry off-screen as well. Jillian tried not to think about that part. It was all a part of the past, just like the people she had loved, or thought she had loved, were a part of her past. At least that's what she kept telling herself as she sat across from her reeling husband.

John looked like he'd been run over by a truck. She had some idea of how he must be feeling. She remembered back to her first night in John's employ, when she found out that the Mr. Romano she was working for was John D. Romano, whom she had had a crush on as a nineteen-year-old nursing student, and who had worked with Monica Morgan, whose character inspired her to go to medical school. Medical school had resulted in her developing an infatuation with a professor, a night of unguarded passion, an unplanned pregnancy, and a huge change in her life's course.

On that first night in the little cobblestone cottage, she had wondered why God had brought her to this place and put her in such a predicament. This "predicament" led her to the life she now had and her marriage to the most special person she had ever known. She figured that God may not have planned every detail, but she believed that God helped it all come out all right in the end. She guessed that she and John had to trust that God would do the same in this current situation, too.

"You want me to do this—with *her*?" John asked. Jillian could hear a mixture of hurt and anger in the way he said that last word. She was not used to this side of John anymore, as he had been such a happy person for almost a year now, ever since their relationship began to develop.

She suddenly felt that perhaps this was something that needed to be addressed in John's life, a hurt from his past that had to be dealt with, once and for all. She remembered seeing Monica Morgan's autobiographical book in the trash can in the garage on one of the first nights she had worked at the house. John had obviously been very hurt by this person, and Jillian knew all too well what that felt like. It had taken her many years to get over the two men who hurt her, and to forgive them. And if she was honest, there were still times when she had to work on that last item, although they rarely came to mind anymore since John became a part of her life.

Again, Jillian felt like she was watching and listening from outside of herself as she said, "I think you should at least give it serious consideration. Sleep on it."

"I doubt that's going to happen." John put his head in his hands. After a few moments he spoke.

"Let's take a walk," he said. "I need some air."

Jillian remembered again the times when she had to face her "demons," as she called them. She often felt the same way she thought John was feeling at the moment. She decided that she would just be silent and let him talk if he wanted, or not if he didn't want to. They walked their familiar two-mile route, holding hands in silence.

It was starting to get dark out when they returned to the house, the days getting shorter and shorter as they closed in on the holiday season. Jillian made a quick salad for dinner, and they ate quietly at the breakfast nook.

Finally John broke the silence. "I just can't believe it. I finally find the perfect script, with the perfect director."

"It's still the same script and the same director," Jillian replied.

"But Monica Morgan...of all people," he said, shaking his head.

"Maybe she's changed," Jillian suggested hopefully.

"I doubt it," John replied bluntly.

"Well, I know I've changed. I know you've changed. We're both a new creation, maybe she is, too," she said.

"You give her too much credit." He paused. "I wish I could be as optimistic as you are," he said finally.

"I don't know if I'm optimistic. I just know I've seen some pretty miraculous things happen in people's lives, including my own."

"You are such a good person," he said, taking her hands, rubbing his fingers over hers.

"So are you," she responded.

"I don't feel like one at the moment," he said honestly.

"Well, I wouldn't have married you if you weren't. So, there!"

"You are way too easy on me, Mrs. Romano," he said, a little bit of the sparkle returning to his eyes.

John was right about not being able to sleep. He stood at the windows of their bedroom suite for a long time. It pained Jillian to see him so troubled. She didn't know what to do or say, so she prayed. She said her usual prayers for her daughter. She prayed that she would be a helper to someone, and on this night for her to help John however she was able. Lastly, she prayed that God would give John what he needed—even if that included hashing out the past with his former lover. It took every bit of strength for Jillian to pray that way. She loved John more than life itself, and the thought of anything—or anyone—hurting her husband, or worse, taking him away from her, was almost more than she could bear. She had to put all her trust in the Lord on this one.

John finally crawled into bed and snuggled up to her back, putting his arm around her. She put her hand on his arm and pulled it tightly around her.

"I didn't know you were still awake," he said quietly.

"I was just praying," she replied.

"Good idea," he said.

She turned over toward John. The moonlight was shining on his face. He looked so tired and distraught. He had been so excited about this role and movie, and now all of this.

She caressed his face. "How about a nurse's massage while I continue my praying?" she offered.

"Would you?" he asked, seeming desperate for some relief.

"I would," she said.

He kissed her softly on the lips. "You are so good to me, Jillian..." It sounded like he wanted to say more, but was at a loss for words. He put his hand on top of her hand that was on his cheek. "I'll love you forever," he said, repeating their nightly refrain.

"I'll love you forever," she responded, and they kissed each other good night.

John turned onto his stomach, and Jillian began to massage his shoulders and upper back. His muscles were tight as she began to work them, but soon she felt his body begin to relax, then his breathing slowed as sleep finally came.

"Thank you, God, for sleep. Now give him—give *us*—your peace," she said quietly out loud, her hand still on his back. Then she kissed him lightly, before drifting off to sleep.

Alan was astonished when John came in to sign the contract late the next morning.

"I thought for sure you'd back out," Alan said as he handed John the papers and a pen.

"It's a great role, a great movie, a great director, and I've got a great wife. That's a lot of *great*, and I'm banking on it that all of that will counter the *not so great*," John relayed.

"I hope you're right." Alan paused for a moment. "Who would have guessed?" he asked, wagging his head back and forth at the irony of it all.

"Not me. Not in a million years. But it is what it is. I'll make it work," John said, trying to sound positive, and trying even harder to convince himself of his own words.

Chapter Six

Two days before Jillian's book was released, Karen called in a frenzy of excitement, with a little bit of fear mixed in for good measure.

"Jillian! He's coming! Our foster son! He's coming home with me after school today. All the paperwork is complete, and we passed all the requirements. Robert has one of our spare bedrooms all fixed up for him. We asked him if he liked sports, and he said 'yes,' especially baseball. He loves the Dodgers. Jillian, I've never seen my husband like this before. He bought all kinds of Dodger items for the room, including a life-sized figure of a player for the wall, bedding, a lamp, some bathroom items, and a bat, ball, and gloves for both of them. I think he went down to the stadium merchandise shop and bought them out!"

Jillian could hear the amazement in her friend's voice. In some ways, it was just like they were bringing a new baby home, except that this was not a permanent situation—at least not at the present time. The boy's father was still in the hospital. The man was an alcoholic and a diabetic—a deadly combination. His internal organs were not in very good shape, particularly his liver and kidneys. He was in serious condition, and Karen had been told he might improve or he might make a huge turn for the worse. If that happened, it would be unlikely that he would survive. The county social worker was working diligently, but still had not located any other family members and was doubtful that there were any.

"Jillian, would you and John come over tomorrow night for dinner? It might be too much for tonight, but we'd really like you to meet him," Karen said.

Jillian imagined that her friend would also like some type of support in this new parenting venture. Karen had to be nervous. Jillian remembered how scared she was when she brought Marty home from the hospital, and she had had her parents there for support and guidance.

"I will check with John to make sure, but I think we can make it," Jillian said. "I'll call you back to confirm. What can we bring?"

"Just yourselves. And your wisdom about kids! We've never had a little boy before," she said, sounding unsure.

"You'll be great foster parents. There's a good reason this young man wanted to live with you," she replied.

"You think so?"

"No, Karen. I *know* so," Jillian said.

The next evening, John and Jillian arrived at Karen's with flowers for the new foster parents, and a tin of baseball cards for their new foster son. Jillian was sorry that in all the excitement, she hadn't even asked for the boy's name, and didn't remember if Karen had ever mentioned it. It had been a wild couple of weeks, and her mind had been preoccupied ever since John had signed his new movie contract.

Karen met them at the door, a huge smile on her face. It was obvious that things had gone well during their first twenty-four

Kathy J. Jacobson

hours of parenting.

"The guys will be out here in a moment. Our young man is a bit shy and needs a little coaxing to come out to meet you. Please don't take it personally—he's had a very tough life and hasn't had much of an example in the area of socialization skills," Karen explained.

"We understand," Jillian said, handing her the flowers. They could hear footsteps slowly approaching.

Robert appeared first, and behind him a smaller body was trying to stay hidden.

Robert stepped aside and spoke, "John and Jillian, this is our foster son, Ri..."

"Rick!" both John and Jillian exclaimed at the same time.

The boys eyes widened in amazement, then a huge smile crossed his face. Then he did something even more incredible. He went over to John and gave him a hug.

Karen and Robert were dumbfounded. "You know one another?" Karen asked after a moment.

"We met last Christmas, at the community dinner at St. Anthony's. We had dinner with Rick and his..." Jillian said, but didn't finish the sentence. She was thinking about the loud, gruff, and abusive man who had yelled at this sweet boy—Ricardo, who liked to be called "Rick"—in front of a room full of people, calling him "stupid" after he accidentally dropped a tray of dirty dishes. John had saved the day by dropping his own tray on purpose, telling Rick that it could happen to anyone, and then John, Jillian, and Rick had cleaned up the messes together.

Rick stood back and then hugged Jillian, too. Then he retreated to Robert's side. It was evident that he was already bonding with his new father figure. Somewhat knowing the father that he had grown up with, it was easy to understand Rick's eagerness to live with people like Karen and Robert.

"Let's all sit down for a minute," Robert said, putting his arm gently around Rick's shoulder.

They went into the living room and sat down on the couches that faced each other, the same ones where many book club discussions had ensued. They talked about meeting one another at the dinner, leaving out the embarrassing details. Jillian thought she may have told Karen about that day last winter, but she wasn't sure. They would have to talk in private about it at a more appropriate time.

"So, you like to be called 'Rick'?" Robert asked, turning to the boy, whose dark bangs kept falling into his even darker eyes.

Rick nodded tentatively.

"Don't ever be afraid to tell us what you like, or don't like, *Rick*," Robert continued, putting emphasis on the boy's preferred name.

Jillian watched the boy's surprised face. She was pretty sure that Rick had never been told anything like that by his own father in his entire life.

"Okay," Rick said, then smiled a shy smile.

John handed Rick the tin of baseball cards. "These are for you. There ought to be a Dodger or two in there somewhere," he said, smiling.

"Thank you," Rick replied, seemingly overwhelmed by all the kindnesses being bestowed upon him.

"Let's open them," Robert suggested, then looked at Karen to see if that was okay with her.

She was soaking in the scene, watching Rick sit between her husband and John, two wonderful men. She nodded her head, her eyes starting to water.

"Jillian, perhaps you could help me in the kitchen for a moment," she said.

"I'd love to," Jillian answered, her own eyes beginning to cloud.

The two women walked into the kitchen. After the door closed behind them, they looked at each other, tears in their eyes, and wrapped their arms around each other in a huge embrace.

"What are the chances?" Karen asked Jillian.

Jillian had asked herself that question quite a bit in the last week or so. She was beginning to see a pattern, and she was perceiving it as a sign that some of the unusual occurrences of late were somehow meant to be. The current situation actually made her feel better, more hopeful, about everything else going on in her life right then.

"I don't think it's chance, Karen. It's a gift. I think everything is going to work out really well, and when I get a feeling like that, it tends to happen," she said, meaning every word.

"I'm starting to get that feeling myself," Karen said, drying her eyes and smiling.

The two women composed themselves and put a plate of appetizers together to take to the living room.

When they came out with the trays of food and beverages, their hearts were warmed again at the sight of the three "men" looking over and discussing the rows of baseball cards that covered the usually pristine coffee table. Jillian thought that Rick wasn't going to be the only one who would have to make adjustments in his lifestyle. Karen and Robert were going to have to learn how messy life could be as parents, in so many different ways.

Rick pointed at a card. "He got traded, but he used to be one of my favorites!"

"Juan Uribe?" Robert asked.

"Sí. I mean 'yes,'" Rick answered.

"Rick, it's okay to speak Spanish," Robert said. "Maybe you could teach me some words. That would be very helpful in my work," he said.

"Really?"

"Sí," said Robert, making Rick smile widely.

"Your name would be Roberto," Rick said to Robert. "And you would be Juan," he said, turning to John. "Just like Juan Uribe!"

Karen and Jillian hated to interrupt them. They put the trays on a nearby table, where Karen often served the book club members.

Robert, John, and Rick decided to take a break and went to check out the food. Jillian noticed that Rick took only a few crackers. She wasn't sure he knew what to make of the rest of the fancy pâtés and dips Karen had prepared. That was going to be another area in which Karen would have to make adjustments and become more educated. Jillian wondered what Karen was serving for dinner, and if it would be something that Rick would want to eat.

Dinner was served about an hour later, and Jillian got her answer. Karen had made a wonderful fish dish, with vegetables on the side. It looked like something from a top-tier restaurant, but not like something a young boy would enjoy.

Rick pushed the food around on his plate for a while and tried to take tiny bites. He gulped down his milk and looked for something on the table that he might like.

Karen noticed and asked him if everything was okay. He started to say "yes," but changed his mind.

"Is it really okay to say if I don't like something?" he asked.

Jillian's heart was breaking, especially when she thought of how badly he had been treated by his father in public several times on Christmas Day. When Rick had tried to carry on a conversation with John and Jillian during dinner, his father had told him to "shut up and eat." She remembered wondering what went on at home as they left the church basement last December the 25th. The thought still mortified her.

"Of course," said Karen.

"I don't really eat fish. Well, maybe fish sticks sometimes at school, but not this kind of fish. I'm sorry," he said, his eyes lowered.

"Well, let's find something else for you to eat," Karen answered, motioning to Rick to join her. The two headed to the kitchen.

"Jillian, maybe you should go and help out," Robert said. "You probably know better what kids like to eat," he said.

Jillian didn't want to invade their special time together, but she thought Robert may have a valid point. She quietly peeked into the kitchen, where every cupboard was open as Karen searched for something that would appeal to a ten-year-old.

"Need any help in here?" Jillian finally asked.

"Yes, that would be nice," Karen said, a panicked look on her face. "I'm afraid we don't have much to offer until we can go shopping together tomorrow."

Jillian thought back to what she and Marty would make if they were tired or running low on supplies in the house. Often they would have "breakfast for supper."

"Do you have flour, eggs, oil, and milk? And how about syrup?"

"Yes, I think we do. What do you suggest?"

"Rick, do you like pancakes?"

The boys eyes got big. "I've only had them a few times, but I *loved* them!"

"Okay, let's whip some up."

Jillian set the two of them to gathering ingredients, then showed them how she and Marty used to make a simple, basic recipe.

The three of them rejoined Robert and John, who were almost done with their dinners, Rick proudly carrying a plate with a tall stack of pancakes on it.

"Man," Robert said, "if I had known that was an option, I wouldn't have eaten all this fish!"

Rick smiled and dug into the pancakes.

"Next time we'll have a pancake party," Karen said, smiling gratefully at Jillian.

"Yes!" Rick exclaimed loudly.

They all laughed at that, and planned when they should have their party. The rest of the evening flew by, filled with chatter about baseball and school. Rick's favorite subject was reading, which made Karen feel good, as she was his reading teacher. Rick was impressed when Robert told him that John had been a college quarterback, and John promised to teach him how to throw a spiral. John also told Rick that he had majored in "reading" in college, but there they called it literature. Rick seemed equally impressed by that.

By ten o'clock, Rick was fading fast. That was okay with Jillian, as her book was going to be released the next day. She was scheduled to do a brief presentation and present a copy to a library in the morning. Then came her formal book launch and signing at a downtown Los Angeles bookstore in the afternoon. She was excited, but was surprised that it seemed to take second place right now to the miraculous thing God was doing right in front of her eyes, in the lives of some special friends—Karen, Robert, and Rick. It had been a night filled with the unexpected. It had been joyous and hopeful, and Jillian left Karen and Robert's feeling ready for anything.

Chapter Seven

Jillian's heart was beating rapidly as she walked up the steps to the library, and not because she was out of shape, which was not the case. Instead, a mixture of excitement and nerves was coursing through her body.

She had done many presentations in the last few years of her nursing career, but never had she presented something that was entirely of her own doing—her own brainchild, her own work, her passion of the past year-and-a-half.

The librarian met her with a smile and led her to a table.

"You may set up your books to sell and sign here, and we have a small stand ready for the one you will present to me after the presentation. We are so excited that you have chosen our little library as your first stop," said the pleasant woman, who Jillian thought to be in her mid-thirties.

"I am happy to be here," Jillian replied, putting down a heavy box of books. "I have more in my car if we need them." She nodded toward the door, then did a double-take when she noticed Pete coming through it and heading right toward her.

"Need any help?" he asked.

"Pete! What in the world? Is everything all right with Kelly and the babies?"

"They're all fine. Kelly is with them now, but I came to get an autographed book from my good friend, Jillian. My daughter's named after the author, you know," he said with a wink.

Jillian felt so honored, and felt pressure building behind her eyes as she stepped closer to give him a hug.

"If you would like me to get those books you were talking about, I'd be happy to," he said.

"We probably won't need more than one more box, if even that. You're a saint, Pete," she said. Jillian took the keys to her Land Rover out of her pocket and handed them over.

Jillian opened the box of books she had brought, along with a number of new pens, a pad of paper to test them on, and some special bookmarks she had made especially for the occasion. She couldn't help but wonder if anyone really came to these types of events. She had sent out invitations to a number of people, the library had advertised it, and she had sent some information to some medical and psychology clinics and a couple of churches in the immediate area, thinking that someone might be interested. Her publisher also sent out some information, but mostly for the bookstore signing that afternoon downtown.

The presentation was set for 10:00 a.m. She had gotten there quite early, not knowing how much time she would need to get ready. She still had forty-five minutes before she talked about the book, answered questions, and handed over a copy to the librarian. She hoped it wasn't going to be just her and Pete in attendance.

Pete came back into the room, a box of books in each arm, making them seem like they were empty rather than filled with heavy books.

"I'm thinking positive," he said as he set them down on the floor next to the table. "Just in case."

As if on cue, a group of people came into the library and looked around. One of them spotted Pete and spoke very loudly, "Hey, Pete! Is this the right place?"

The librarian shushed the man who had spoken. Pete nodded. The group of very physically fit individuals took seats. Just as they did, another group of people walked in. She recognized a couple of them as staff from the hospital where the babies were currently residing in the NICU, including a cleaning woman, a CNA, and a couple of nurses.

Some other people came in whom Jillian didn't know, and who didn't seem to know Pete either. Then came Greta and Drew, which surprised Jillian as it was only six days until their wedding.

They came over to her and hugged her. "Congrats, Jillian," Greta said with a big smile on her face.

"It's so nice of you both to come," Jillian told them.

"I had to see what was so important to you that you would take a job as a housekeeper," Drew said. He never had completely understood the "what" or "why" of Jillian's move and new career choices.

Greta elbowed him sharply.

"I mean, I'm happy that all of your hard work has paid off," he said. They headed to the chairs, Drew uttering a little "ouch" under his breath.

Jillian couldn't believe the influence Greta had on Drew. She seemed to be able to say, or do, anything to him, and he would actually listen to her and try harder. Jillian was so happy that he found someone who could help him become a better person, the person she always thought he could be. She and Drew had dated on and off for almost a year, but it was clear from the start that Jillian was certainly *not* the right person to help make that happen.

The couple took seats in the front row, Drew still rubbing his ribs where Greta had poked him. Pete sat down in the back, so as to not block the view of anyone who might be unfortunate enough to sit behind his massive form.

Others came in, including a book club group, and another group of women from a church in the neighborhood. Before Jillian knew it, almost all the chairs in the area were filled. The librarian, knowing Jillian had another engagement in the afternoon, promptly introduced her at 10:00 a.m. sharp. Jillian silently said a prayer and then stood up to tell the people the story of her project, as she often thought of it.

She spoke for about twenty minutes, reading some excerpts from the book, then answered questions. The women from the book club and church group commented that they were happy that there were questions for discussion at the end of each chapter. Others asked about the blog. Some asked what inspired her. They all seemed so interested, and Jillian found it an enjoyable experience.

The people from the hospital were impressed that there were actually scenarios with which they were familiar, and were eager to share information about the book and blog with their co-workers.

At the end, Jillian presented the library with a free, autographed copy of the book, and then proceeded to sell and sign almost all the books she had in the building.

"Good thing you brought in both boxes, Pete," Jillian said. "Who were your friends who came? They bought a lot of books!"

"They are other people in my business. I informed them that physical health is often linked to emotional health, and told them they should check out your book, and promote it in their clubs."

"You are a sweetheart," she said.

"Jillian, I could never repay you for all the ways you have helped me, and my family," he told her, saying that last part with the pride of a new father.

"Pete, you don't need to repay me for anything. Just having you, and your *family*," she said, putting an emphasis on that word, "as my friends, is repayment enough."

Jillian started to put away the few books she had left.

"Wait, I want to buy a couple of those," he said.

"You don't have to buy them," she replied.

"I want to buy them, please. I need two. One made out to Kelly and me, the other one made out to Grace Jillian," he said with a smile.

She sat down and wrote a thoughtful note in each, along with her signature. Her hand was already getting stiff, and she was grateful she had a few hours before she had to start signing again. Maybe there wouldn't be many people at the bookstore. One just never knew about these things.

Jillian was pleasantly surprised by the steady stream of people who had lined up at the bookstore to have a copy of the book signed. Her publisher and agent had no doubt done a good job of promoting it. She was also aware that it probably didn't hurt that some people knew she was married to a celebrity, and one who was regaining star status at an increasingly rapid rate.

Jillian had wanted John to come today, but he was wise enough to know that it would not be a good idea. After she thought about it, she knew he was right. It was getting more and more difficult for them to do anything in public, and she knew it was going to get a thousand times worse after news and promotion of his new movie began, which would be happening shortly.

One of the most pleasant surprises of the afternoon was the arrival of her own book club members, led by Karen.

"I thought you and Rick would be out shopping today," Jillian said as her friend approached.

"Oh, don't worry, we filled two carts this morning! I've never had so much fun grocery shopping, and I bought a lot of things I've never even heard of before. Now Rick and Robert are out looking for a Dodgers baseball jersey. Robert is in heaven, and so am I," her friend said, a sparkle in her eye that Jillian had never seen before.

Jillian smiled as she wrote a message and signed the book, then sent up a prayer as Karen stepped aside for the next person in line. She prayed that the story of Karen, Robert, and Rick would have a happy ending, and sincerely hoped that her good friends would not have their hearts broken again.

After an hour, the worker announced that the signing would soon be ending, but to watch for another event soon. Jillian couldn't believe how quickly time had gone, or how sore her hand was.

She stood up and began to put her pens away when the manager came over to her and whispered in her ear.

"There's one more person who would like a book signed."

Jillian looked around, but the line had dissipated.

"Come with me," he said in a low voice, and she followed him to a door that had a sign on it which read *Employees Only*. Jillian guessed it must be the person's boss, to rate a private signing.

"Here you go," the man said, opening the door for her. She stepped in, and the door closed behind her. She was confused when the man didn't come in with her, but then she turned and saw why.

There, holding one of her books and a pen, with that familiar grin that melted her heart, was the beaming face of her husband.

"May I have your autograph?" John asked.

"Sorry, time's up," she said teasingly, putting her hands on John's hands, which held the book and pen.

"Please?" he asked.

"Maybe—for a kiss," she said.

"I can handle that," he answered, wrapping his arms—book, pen, and all—around her and pulling her into a deep, passionate kiss.

Jillian sighed a deep sigh of pleasure as John held her in his arms afterward. She didn't want him to ever let go. He seemed more handsome and desirable than ever. He was back in great physical shape, and had a new look thanks to the studio's hair and makeup artists. They gave him a new, more modern hairstyle, as well as having him keep a very slight growth of his beard during the filming. Monica, when she saw him at a meeting with the director, proclaimed she "hated it," and was already complaining about having to kiss him with that "stubble" on his face. But Jillian liked it, and Marty, when she saw him on a video call, said it was "hot."

"Thank you for coming, John," she said softly, stroking the roughness of his face.

"I'm so proud of you, Jillian," he said, and kissed her on the forehead. "I peeked out the door. You had quite the crowd out there. How did this morning go?"

"It was a great—better than expected," she said.

"Wonderful. Let's go and celebrate."

"Okay. How should we do this?"

"Well, the manager is guarding the door until you go back out. I suppose you ought to take your car and meet me. Where do you want to go?"

"Leo's," she said, the restaurant they went to on their first date, and later had their wedding dinner.

"Great idea. I'll call him and tell him we're coming," he said, and kissed her once more. "And Jillian, you still need to sign my book."

He held out the pen and the book. It reminded her of the day she'd almost left John's house, and him. He had handed her the note telling her to stay, then a note pad and pen for her response. Now she took the book and pen from him and wrote.

I'll love you forever, John.
Jillian

He looked at it and smiled. "Perfect," he said, then clutched the book to his chest. "I'll meet you at Leo's," he said.

She kissed him once more.

"What was that for?" he asked.

"For being you," she said.

John had escaped out the back door of the manager's office, wearing a hat and sunglasses. His Land Rover was parked down the street, and he hopped in just as he saw someone pointing at him. Luckily, no one was coming down the street at that moment, and he was able to quickly and safely pull away from the curb and be on his way. He was excited about all his recent new acting opportunities, but he was not excited about some of the other inevitable hazards he knew were in store for him and Jillian because of them.

John and Jillian enjoyed their usual pasta and pizza at their little table, set aside especially for them by Leo. On the table was a vase with a single yellow rose, which John had ordered on his way over and had paid some ridiculous amount of money to have delivered immediately to Leo's.

Jillian filled John in on the day's events and the friends who were in attendance, her voice filled with excitement and hopefulness. John listened attentively, his face full of love and pride.

Jillian had thought the book events had been enough to celebrate, but seeing John in that back office at the end of the day, with that smile on his face and love in his eyes, was tops. She could barely take her eyes off him the entire evening.

They ended their evening with Leo's incredible tiramisu. After they set down their forks, John took her chin in his hand.

"Where to next, author Jillian Johnson Romano? It's your special day," he said.

"Home," she answered, her eyes glued to his.

"Another great idea," he said softly, tracing the contour of her face with his finger. He flagged down their waiter and handed him some cash. They quickly left through the back door of the restaurant to avoid the line of people at the front entrance, anxious to get home.

They pulled into the garage almost in tandem. John came over and held her door open for her, his book in his hand. Jillian climbed out of her vehicle, and they walked into the house. She threw her purse down on the counter, and John took her hand, gently guiding her down the hallway to the library.

Once inside the room, he carefully set her book on his table where he always put his latest "read." He turned to her and put his arms gently around her waist.

"I've never had the author of one of my books in my library before," he said with a smile, and pulled her close.

"There's a first time for everything, I guess," she replied softly, pulling him even closer. "So, that means you've probably never kissed the author of one of your books in your library before either?"

He gently pushed a wisp of hair back from her face. "No, but as you said, there's a first time for everything." Then his lips met hers.

Chapter Eight

There was barely a chance for a breath between the book release and Drew and Greta's wedding. Jillian had more book signings the day after the release, the next evening, and then a short break before Thanksgiving Day and the ensuing frenzy of "Black Friday."

Jillian had spoken with Greta the day after the book talk at the library to get any last-minute instructions for the ceremony. What a refreshing young woman! She was smart, pretty, independent, calm in some ways, and feisty in others. She didn't seem to be at all phased by the upcoming nuptials.

Greta and Drew were going to be married in the backyard of Greta's parents' home, an adobe-style house completely powered by solar energy and other alternative energy sources, near the Los Angeles River and the Sepulveda Dam. Greta's father owned and ran an alternative energy business, and Greta had mentioned that their home was a showcase of his work. John and Jillian had hired him to the do the solar projects on their property. Jillian was excited to see the house, to meet Greta's mom, and see what sounded like a unique setting for a wedding.

The big day arrived in no time at all. The backyard was even more special than Jillian had anticipated, private and filled with beautiful trees that she had never seen before. She was informed that they were Arroyo Willows, native to the area. They made a stunning backdrop for the ceremony.

Jillian thought that Drew and Greta might have a judge officiate, but the associate pastor, Pastor Katie, from Drew's parents' church, was there to preside. It was a simple but beautiful service. Jillian and John had little to do except sign the marriage license and hold a bouquet of flowers and produce the wedding bands, respectively. Considering their crazy schedules of late, both were very appreciative of their simple roles.

Drew and Greta had written their own vows to each other. Jillian saw a side of Drew that she had never witnessed before, one that was both compassionate and attentive. It was so clearly evident that these two people were meant to be together and become husband and wife.

Jillian was not only pleasantly surprised by Drew's vows to Greta, but by the way the two families seemed to be getting along. Drew's mother, as it turned out, used to paint in high school and had once wanted to be an artist. She hadn't touched a palette in years, but Greta had convinced her to try again and was even giving her some lessons. Greta's mother also loved to grow roses like Drew's mother, which became a common bond between them.

Drew's father was impressed with Greta's father's initiative to get into alternative energy before it became popular. Now that it was becoming increasingly necessary, it appeared to be a great investment, both financially, and for the future of the state, nation, and world. He appeared genuinely interested when John and Jillian told him about their recent energy updates, and mentioned that he should consider doing the same at his home.

The Thanksgiving/wedding dinner was delicious. John particularly liked the tofu turkey, and Jillian enjoyed the tofu coconut curry, which were served along with Drew's family's traditional turkey dinner fixings. It was the only time Jillian remembered having pumpkin pie as a "wedding cake." She thought it was one of the best wedding dinners she had ever had, second only to their own at Leo's.

They all stood outside in the late afternoon sun and waved goodbye to Drew and Greta as they drove off. They were going on a brief honeymoon through Sunday night. Greta had school on Monday, and Drew was in the midst of an important project at work. He was also helping John and Jillian tremendously with getting the acting school set up financially. He was very good at his profession. Jillian thought he should be, considering how much time he spent working. She wondered if things would change after Greta was finished with graduate school. She may not want her husband at the office all day and night once she didn't have to study so much.

Greta couldn't wait to be done with school. This was her last full semester of classes. Next semester, she would have two classes and finish her dissertation, defend it to the faculty, and have it approved. Drew had surprised Greta with the gift of a future home studio. Jillian was quite sure that he had saved a lot of money over the years. He also owned his own home, which Greta told Jillian they were planning to sell. They hoped to buy, or possibly build, something else in the coming year, after they knew where Greta might be working. They would look for a place with room to add on a studio for her pottery and other art projects. Greta had been blown away by his kind gesture.

Greta had sculpted a lovely piece of the two of them in an embrace, which he planned to put on a shelf in his office. Drew had

Kathy J. Jacobson

proudly shown it off to the wedding guests, with tears of joy in his eyes.

It was a Thanksgiving none of those in attendance would soon forget, full of reminders of all the things and people they loved, and for which they were very thankful.

On the way home, John and Jillian drove past a grassy field where a game of cricket was in progress. Some people enjoyed football on Thanksgiving, but in this area, the English game was popular.

Seeing the people outside after their holiday dinners made John and Jillian decide to stop and walk for a bit in the wildlife refuge area. The cricket pitch had been busy with players and fans, but the refuge was quiet and still in comparison.

They held hands as they meandered, coming to a halt to look at an impressive area of indigenous wildflowers. John turned to Jillian and pulled her into an embrace, holding her tightly. "That was a nice wedding," he said.

"Almost as nice as ours," she replied.

"Almost."

"I am sure happy that Drew found Greta," Jillian said.

"And I'm even happier that Drew found Greta," he responded, his eyes penetrating hers.

Jillian smiled at that. "I don't think you had anything to worry about, John. Drew was never the one for me. You were.

"I'm glad," he said, moving even closer to her.

"Me, too," she said, running her hand along the side of his face. "This is our first Thanksgiving together." She paused. "I've never felt more thankful in my entire life."

"Neither have I. I wish there was some way I could show you how very thankful I am—for you," he said, then kissed her tenderly.

"Well, that's a good start."

The first order of business when they arrived home was to call Tommy and Maria to wish them a Happy Thanksgiving. They had already talked to Marty early in the morning, as it was nine hours ahead where she was living. Both mother and daughter were getting what Jillian referred to as "short-timers blues." Jillian wanted Marty home—now. Marty had already begun to pack things up and would be home in just shy of three weeks. In the meantime, Marty was happy to be busy saying goodbye to good friends and tying up the loose ends of her work, and Jillian was happy to be very busy with her book adventures as well. It helped the time go a little bit faster.

John and Jillian sat on the love seat in the library and put the phone on speaker. Tommy and Maria gave a very positive report from their front. It had been a fun season of college football. John Anthony's team was doing well. He ended up "redshirting," which wasn't a bad idea for his first year. It gave him time to develop his skills and fill out physically. It also gave him more time to devote to his studies in the musical theater program. He had worked backstage on one of the musical theater productions in the fall, and had high hopes for the second semester to make it onto the stage.

Alison was a top student in her large class, and particularly excelled in science and math. She was beginning to look at colleges already and making a list of those she wanted to visit. They thought that they might take a vacation during the summer and hit a few of the prospects that were near one another.

Maria's new business was booming. Apparently, everyone else enjoyed the Romano family recipes just as much as they did. She had so many orders for Thanksgiving, she almost had to turn some customers away. Maria planned to hire Alison to help with small tasks at Christmas and was going to hire someone else to cook

Kathy J. Jacobson

with her. They reported that unfortunately there was no way they would be able to come to California for Christmas, New Year's, or Easter for that matter. Holidays were huge days for someone in Maria's business.

John and Jillian suggested they start looking at the calendar and pick some dates to visit, and see if they could coordinate around book tours and the movie production. They "made a plan to make a plan," as John put it.

Toward the end of the conversation, Tommy asked if he could speak with just Jillian for a moment. John said his goodbye and his "I love you" to his beloved nephew, and then handed the phone to Jillian. She took it off speaker mode and spoke into the phone.

"Hi, Tommy!" She absolutely adored the man.

"Jillian—I thought I'd call you back later, but I just had to tell you!" he whispered excitedly. Jillian thought perhaps he was afraid that John was standing nearby and might overhear him, which was an accurate assumption. "I found it—the family crèche!"

Her eyes widened, and she was going to blurt something out, but realized that Tommy had asked to talk to her alone and obviously didn't want it revealed to John yet. She let him continue.

"One of my father's best friends from Belvidere called me a few days ago and asked if I was ever going to come and get the boxes and trunk belonging to my father that were in his garage. He is hoping to put his house up for sale and move into a condo, and needed to get the house ready to show. I knew nothing of a trunk or boxes.

"Apparently, my father asked his friend to store them when he knew he was getting sick, knowing that he was going to have to go into memory care at some point. But unfortunately, my father forgot to ever mention it to me. So, last night I drove over and retrieved the items. And there, in the trunk, was the crèche. It looks— just like I remember it," he said, his voice filled with emotion.

"That's wonderful, Tommy," Jillian said.

"I want you to give it to John for Christmas," he told her.

"Tommy, are you sure?" she asked, not wanting to say too much as John was still in the room.

"I am positive. I will get my turn someday, hopefully. In the meantime, I want Zio to have it. He loved it so much. I know you gave him the snow globe that was like it last year. He showed it to me. That was so thoughtful of you. But this year, I want you to give him the real thing on Christmas Day. Email me later, and we'll make a plan to get it out there without him finding out," he said.

"Will do," she replied, so excited at the prospect of giving John something so precious and special to him for Christmas, but trying to sound nonchalant. She was trying to think about what she would tell John when he asked what Tommy wanted, but just then John's cell phone went off in another room, and she was spared having to concoct an explanation.

"Thanks so much, Tommy," she said after John was out of earshot. "I will make sure that it is specified that it be returned to you, or one of your children in the future."

"Thanks, Jillian. Happy Thanksgiving!" he said.

"Yes, it's a very happy one. All my love to all of you," she replied.

"Same to you, Jillian. Thanks again, for everything. I'm so glad you are a part of our family."

Jillian's eyes teared up. "So am I... So am I."

While Drew and Greta were off honeymooning, John was learning his lines for the movie, which would begin with a read-through on Monday, and Jillian signed book after book at five different stores.

She also did a brief signing session between church services at Grace Lutheran. Nancy had set up the event, wanting the church family to support Jillian in her new career. Leave it to Nancy to be so thoughtful. Almost the entire Bible study group bought one, along with Pastor Jim and many others. Jillian donated one to the church library for those who were not able to afford a copy.

One of her friends from the Bible study said he bought one for his "little sister," who had recently lost her husband of thirty-seven years. Jillian kept forgetting how many people had a loss in their lives, sometimes more than one they were dealing with at a time. She was beginning to see her new work as just as important as her old. It was just a different way of helping others heal.

As Jillian was beginning to pack up the box of books at church, Nancy came over from where she and Buck had been standing and talking with John.

"Is it too late for me to get a book?" she asked.

Jillian had been so busy that she didn't even notice that Nancy had not had one signed.

"Of course not. It's never too late for you, Nancy. And thank you so much for setting this up today. It was sweet of you, and it was nice to be here today before life gets even crazier for John and me," she said, picking up a book and opening it to the front pages.

Nancy started digging into her purse.

"Don't even think about it, Nancy," Jillian said.

Jillian wrote a special message to one of her first friends at church, the woman who was as tall on faith and love as she was short in stature. She handed it to Nancy. Nancy grabbed it and held it tightly to her chest, like it was treasure.

"I'll cherish it forever," she said.

Just then Jillian noticed a flash of brilliance coming from Nancy's left hand, and focused in on one of the largest, most elaborate diamond rings she had ever seen.

"Nancy!" was all Jillian could say.

Nancy smiled a huge smile. "I wondered if I was going to have to stand on my head for you to notice it," she said.

"I can't believe I didn't see something that amazing from all the way across the room. It's so beautiful! I am so happy for you both," Jillian said, and looked over at Buck who was deep in conversation with John.

Jillian stood up and hugged her friend, then the two of them walked over to the men.

"Congratulations, Buck!" Jillian said, and hugged the tall, rugged rancher.

"It's y'all's fault, you know, gettin' married last Easter, and being so in love and everything," he said. "Makes a man get crazy ideas like gettin' married himself."

Nancy held out her hand to John to show him her ring.

He whistled. "That's some ring! Congratulations, both of you," he said, and hugged Nancy and shook Buck's hand.

"We're goin' to get married the Sunday before Christmas—during the late service. Nancy's kids and grandkids will all be home that weekend. We're goin' to have our family Christmas dinner and gifts on Saturday, and everyone's bringin' and servin' the food, so we just get to sit back and enjoy ourselves. Then after church we're goin' to go out to brunch—takin' up an entire room at some fancy restaurant!"

"We'd love it if you both could join us," Nancy said.

Jillian checked her phone planner quickly. It looked like she would be at an area bookstore later that afternoon, but nothing in the morning. She looked at John, who was looking at his phone calendar.

"I think it will work for me, too, barring any schedule changes," he said.

Buck and Nancy stood with their arms around each other's backs, Nancy's arm stretched as far up as she could make it go.

They made the most unusual couple—he was so tall, and even taller with his cowboy hat and boots, and she was so petite. But at that moment, they looked absolutely *perfect* together.

Early that evening, after hours of reading excerpts, signing books at a bookstore and then driving home, Jillian dragged herself into the kitchen. The room was filled with the wonderful aroma of homemade lentil chili that John was making, along with a pan of corn bread which sat cooling on the counter.

John stood at the stove with a long wooden spoon in his hand.

"Thank you so much, John. I didn't know what we were going to do for dinner tonight, and I didn't really feel like going out," she said, hugging him from behind as he stirred the pot of spicy legumes and tomatoes.

"I needed a little break, and this sounded good," he said.

"*You* sound good," she responded, squeezing him tightly and putting the side of her head against his back.

He smiled and exhaled loudly. He turned off the burner and turned to her, pulling her close. "Jillian," he said, and kissed her.

When the kiss ended, she looked into those chocolate-colored eyes and said, "It's y'all's fault—gettin' married, and being so in love and everything."

Chapter Nine

Monday morning came extra early as John had to be at the studio for measurements in the costume department before the reading. Jillian could tell he was both excited and wary. She had to admit those were her exact sentiments as well. She tried to "put the best construction" on the situation, something she had learned about many years ago from both her parents and her pastor during Confirmation class. She was hoping that Monica would not be unkind to John—but not too friendly either.

Jillian had sometimes wondered what would happen if she were to run into Marty's biological father, Dr. Jeffrey Lawrence, or the last man who had broken her heart, former colleague Pastor Scott Bradford. She had spent so many years trying to put both of them out of her mind, and heart. She tried to imagine what John must be feeling like right now, knowing he was not only going to *see* Monica, but had to work with her every day, including "work" comprised of a number of romantic acting scenes.

Jillian knew that John loved her, but she also knew that he was human. She hoped that Monica's marriage was as wonderful as her own. According to Monica's book, which had been published the year before, her husband, Ben, was the love of her life. Jillian was hoping that was still the case, and that Monica would behave like a happily married woman.

It was clear from John's weary sigh when he came home that Jillian's hopes were not the case.

"That bad?" Jillian asked after he hugged her.

"The script is great. The cast is great. The director is great. The irritation is great."

"What happened?" Jillian asked, not certain she really wanted to know.

"Nothing major, I guess. Just a few off-color remarks—innuendo," he said. "All very unprofessional." Noticing the somewhat worried look on Jillian's face, he hugged her again. "I'm sorry to unload on you, Jillian—especially something like that. It's probably about the last thing you want to hear."

Jillian agreed with that last comment, but also knew that John was just being upfront with her.

"That's probably true, but I do appreciate your honesty, John. You could have just said that it was a great day and left it at that."

"I love you too much to do that, Jillian."

"I love you, too, John," she said, and hugged him tightly. She was glad that he couldn't see the hint of concern that was still hanging on in her heart. She hoped that this was a one-time thing, but somehow knew that it probably wasn't going to be that easy.

John and Jillian had just finished the dishes and were heading to the library when Jillian received a call from Karen. Rick's father had just died. She wondered if one or both of them could come over. She looked at her exhausted husband, who had been up since before dawn and was yawning as he picked up her book.

"I'll be over, Karen. I'm not sure about John. He had quite a day and has another early call tomorrow." She put down her cell phone and went over to John, who had just taken a seat on the love seat and was waiting for her to join him there.

"What's up?" John asked.

"Rick's father just passed away. Karen asked if we—or I—could come over for a bit," she said, sitting down next to him. All she really wanted to do was curl up with John and watch him read.

"I'm going with you," he said, closing the book and putting it back in its spot. "I've been gone all day. The only thing I really want to do is be with you." He fingered her hair as she leaned against his shoulder.

She kissed him on the cheek. "I'll get my keys. I'm driving," she said, thinking he might have a chance to rest his eyes. Karen and Robert only lived about ten minutes away, or fifteen if there was traffic, but any chance to relax might be welcomed after a long day like John had had.

She grabbed her key ring from the kitchen counter, along with a container of chocolate chip cookies she had just baked. It was almost like she was supposed to have made them for the occasion. When she was growing up in Wisconsin, if someone had a death in the family, you always took them food. And when a ten-year-old loses his father, it seemed like cookies fit the bill.

Karen, Robert, and Rick met them at the door. Rick didn't hide behind Robert as he had the first time. Again, he hugged both John and Jillian, and they told him how sorry they were about his father.

Rick didn't say anything in response. Jillian knew that he was most likely feeling very conflicted. On the one hand, his father was a mean and abusive man. On the other hand, he was his father and, as far as they knew, his only living relative.

Jillian handed Karen the cookies. They all went into the kitchen and sat around the table. Karen asked if anyone wanted some milk with their cookies.

"Of course," Jillian replied.

"Me, too," said Rick.

Robert put on a small pot of coffee for himself, Karen, and John.

They talked about what had happened that day, and what was going to happen in the coming days. There would be some type of service at the funeral home. While they didn't discuss it at that moment in front of Rick, Karen and Robert were paying for the entire funeral and burial. They didn't want Rick's father put in some kind of "potter's field" somewhere. They wanted Rick to be able to visit his grave if he ever chose to do so.

"We were wondering if your pastor might say a few words at the service," Karen said. "Rick and his father didn't really have a church, but Rick said he thought his father believed in God."

"I'll call him first thing tomorrow morning," Jillian said. "When were you thinking of having the service?"

"Well, we know that John is busy all day almost every day, and Sundays are very busy, so we thought in the late afternoon or early evening sometime this week, whatever works for the pastor and for you two. We would all really like you to be there. The funeral director is flexible," Robert said.

"That's very kind of you. We would be honored to be there," John said, and checked his schedule, which showed his estimated finish times for each day. He actually had one day that didn't go as late as the others, so they said they would try to have a late afternoon service on that day.

They finished their milk, coffee, and cookies. Rick looked tired and sad, John was beat, and Karen and Robert looked concerned for their young charge.

"Karen, I think we should be going, but I'll be in touch with you as soon as I talk to Pastor Jim," she said. "And if you don't mind, I'd like to offer a short prayer." Karen nodded in agreement. They all held hands around the table.

Jillian thanked God for the gift of life, for the life of Rick's father, and prayed that he was in a better place where there were no more troubles, and where he could be a new creation. She also prayed for God's love and peace to be felt by Rick, and all of them. Everyone said, "Amen," and Jillian noticed a tear roll down Rick's cheek, which he quickly wiped away.

Wipe away all his tears from now on, Lord, Jillian prayed to herself.

Everyone hugged goodbye, and Jillian and John headed to her white Land Rover, which they had parked on the street. John clasped her hand in his as they walked down the driveway. Once they arrived at her vehicle, he opened the door for her. Before she hopped in, he put his hands on her shoulders.

"You are one special person, Mrs. Romano," he said. Jillian loved it when he called her that, and he knew it.

"Thank you, and so are you, Mr. Romano" she replied, then kissed him before stepping up into the driver's seat.

John walked around and got into the front passenger seat. Jillian had wondered if the coffee would keep John up all night. She had her answer a minute into the drive home, as he was sound asleep.

Two days later, at 4:30 p.m., in the Peace Chapel of a funeral home, they had a beautiful service for Carlos Walker, Rick's father. Those who attended were Rick, Karen, Robert, John, Jillian, and, at the last minute, a disheveled man who came in and sat in the back row. Rick didn't even see him until he stood up to read some scripture. Jillian had told Rick how people, especially family members, often read Bible passages at funerals. Since he loved reading so much, he wanted to read. So Rick read the Twenty-third Psalm—perfectly. Pastor Jim read from the Gospel of John, then gave a brief, but meaningful message. Then Jillian sang "Amazing Grace," accompanying herself with her guitar. She noticed that Karen was weeping by the end of the song. The words did tend to make people do that.

The man in attendance was Jorge, a friend of Carlos' since childhood. He had heard about the death and funeral down at the homeless shelter where he was residing. It was the same shelter where Rick and his father had stayed whenever they were evicted from an apartment, which was a fairly common occurrence.

The six funeral attendees drove to the cemetery in the Land Rover afterward. Pastor Jim took his own car so he could go home after the graveside prayers. The sun was starting to set as they laid Carlos to rest. It was very peaceful and gave them all a sense of hope that indeed a new day would dawn again.

They were headed back toward the car when Jillian heard Rick's stomach growl. He was a growing boy, and Karen and Robert would have to begin preparing themselves for a big food bill if they were able to have Rick live with them long-term.

"I'm getting hungry," Jillian said as they hopped in.

"Me, too," said Rick. He always seemed to wait for someone else to bring things up, still a bit timid to ask for the things he needed. Jillian was pretty sure that he was often scolded, or worse, whenever he had expressed his needs to his father.

"How about some pancakes?" John asked.

"Yes!" said Rick.

"Jorge, will you join us?" asked Karen, surprising herself a bit.

The ragged man looked equally surprised at being asked. "Yes, thank you, Ma'am."

Jillian got out her cell phone and typed pancake houses into the browser. There was one only blocks away. They found a spot to park, and they all piled out of the vehicle and headed in.

The manager eyed the unusual group of people—five who were clean and all dressed up, and one who looked like he just came off the streets, which was pretty much the case.

During the meal, they found out more about Carlos. Much of it looked like news to Rick. Carlos, whose father was white and mother Latina, had been a star athlete in high school. Rick's mother was a beautiful Latina woman, who had been a cheerleader in high school. They seemed to be the perfect couple, until Carlos got kicked off the team.

Jorge said that Carlos was big and strong, like his dad. He was also smart, but didn't like being smart, so he often did stupid things to try to not be seen as a "goody two-shoes." His only saving grace was his girlfriend, who later became his wife, a sweet young woman named Rita, Rick's mother. Rita, unfortunately, died when Rick was a toddler. Jorge said that after Rita died, Carlos began to drink, and bit by bit, he became more and more like his father.

At that point, Robert said he needed to use the restroom and suggested Rick should join him and wash his hands before they had their meal. Jillian was quite sure that Robert didn't care for the course of the conversation and wanted to spare Rick any more heartache.

It was a good move on his part, as the story of Rick's family took an even worse turn. Jorge continued by saying that Carlos' "old man," meaning Carlos' father, was the meanest man he'd ever known. And then came the bomb.

"Still is," he tacked on. At that, Karen looked like someone shot her. Rick had a living relative—a grandfather.

"He's still living?" she finally got up the nerve to ask.

"I guess you could say that. He's in prison. Life sentence with no parole," he informed them.

"Oh, my," Karen said.

Just then the pancakes came. Rick and Robert returned to the table, and the conversation ended. They all ate with gusto, all except Karen, who had lost her appetite. Later Karen asked Jorge, while Rick was up in front of the restaurant with John and Robert paying the bill, what Carlos' father had done to be incarcerated.

"He murdered his wife," he said bluntly.

Karen and Jillian were both very glad that Rick was not there to learn that his grandfather had killed his grandmother. It was no wonder that Carlos had turned out the way he had.

They dropped Jorge off at a shelter where he said his belongings were stored. Robert slipped him some money and thanked him for joining them. Jillian didn't know how much Robert had handed him, but from the look on Jorge's face, it was pretty significant, or at least it was to him in his current circumstances.

They drove back to the funeral home where Karen and Robert's car was parked. The Wilsons and Rick hugged John and Jillian goodbye, thanked them again, and were on their way. It was, after all, a school night and a work night. But it had been, despite the occasion, a good night. The only downside had been the discovery about Rick's grandfather. They would just have to put that bit of information into God's hands now.

Chapter Ten

The time between Thanksgiving and Christmas felt like someone hit the fast-forward button. With it being the holiday season, many bookstores were interested in promoting books that helped those who had personal losses and struggles, who especially suffered during "the most wonderful time of the year."

Jillian could barely keep up with her schedule, and more and more events were added as time progressed. Most of them were on the weekends, which was unfortunate, as the only time John had off was on Sunday, if he had any at all. At least they had Sunday mornings together. Except for the times when Jillian was out of town, she had asked that her Sunday mornings remain free so she could go to church. Even on the road, she planned to attend worship if at all possible.

During this time, Karen and Robert spent many hours with the social worker, making certain that no family member was available to take care of Rick. The social worker had verified that his paternal grandfather was indeed in prison for life with no parole. She had spoken with him, and told him about his son and grandson. His only response was, "I wouldn't want to take care of some stupid rugrat, even if I was on the outside."

Karen was horrified upon hearing that. Jillian was not surprised, but was certainly saddened. Karen was also worried about Rick. Since his father's death, he had been hoarding some food—not anything major, but things like candy bars, granola bars, and some fruit. Karen had discovered it when she smelled something rotten in his bedroom, and found a molding orange in the corner of Rick's bedroom closet.

Jillian suggested that if he wasn't already doing so, Rick should see a counselor. She could only imagine what kinds of situations he had endured in his short lifetime that might manifest themselves in unhealthy ways if not nipped in the bud. This recent behavior could be a reaction to his father's death, or it might have happened anyway. She thought it best to have a professional make an assessment, and Karen and Robert were thankfully "all in."

Karen and Robert were wonderful foster parents. They wanted the best for Rick, so found help right away. The counselor discovered that Rick was amazingly well-adjusted, considering his personal background. He still had many insecurities, however. Rick had been honest with the counselor about the food hoarding. He said that he was keeping the food in case he had to go back out on the street.

Karen had cried when she heard that. Jillian assured her that it was not because of anything she or Robert had done wrong, but to remember that Rick had ten years of life with a parent on whom he could not rely. It would take some time for him to really trust anyone, even the most loving and caring people like her and Robert. The counselor apparently said pretty much the same thing to them, so they started to feel better and to do everything they could to help Rick feel secure and loved in their home. Jillian didn't think that Rick could do any better than to be in the care of her good friends.

The movie was progressing, and Monica's poor behavior was as well. Her acting was fine. She was very talented, and she and John still had an amazing onscreen chemistry. But offscreen, John could barely tolerate her. Unfortunately, the more he resisted her, the worse her advances became.

The paparazzi didn't help either. Almost immediately, there were photos of the two of them on the front of the gossip magazines. One photo showed them walking out to the parking lot at the end of the filming day with a caption of "*John and Monica—Back in the Saddle Again?*" Several magazines talked about the marital problems that Monica and Ben were supposedly having, and wondered if it was because of John.

Jillian did wonder why Monica was acting this way, as she had spoken so glowingly of her husband, Ben Bastien, and their twin sons, only the year before in her book. Jillian explored the Internet, looking for answers. There were more articles, even prior to the shooting of the movie, which described problems in her marriage, and others that covered the exploits of one of her sons, Brent. He had just been picked up on a charge of drunk driving. Other articles mentioned he also appeared to be out with a different woman every week, including one who was old enough to be his mother. Jillian found herself actually feeling sorry for Monica after reading all the articles.

Her empathy didn't last too long, however. One day early in the week, Jillian went to the movie lot to surprise John with a lunch and some other goodies. It was going to be a marathon day of filming. As she came near his trailer door, she saw Monica come out, throwing back her head and laughing, and saying very loudly, "Let me know when you change your mind!" She stomped off, a look of determination on her face that worried Jillian.

Jillian knocked on the trailer door.

"I told you I'm not interested, Monica!" John barked through the closed door.

"It's me, John," Jillian said.

The door opened. "Jillian!" A smile crossed his tired-looking face, as he pulled her gently into the trailer and into his arms. "This is a wonderful surprise," he said. "Not like my last one."

"I saw Monica leaving," Jillian told him, searching her husband's face.

"What nerve! She knocked on the door and said she *had* to talk to me about something urgent. I thought maybe there was a problem with the script or a scene, or something with her family. I was just trying to be nice—I should have known better. She barged in, threw her arms around me, and even tried to kiss..." He stopped speaking for a moment and hugged her. "I realize that's probably not the kind of news you'd like to hear," he said, pulling back and looking her straight in the eyes.

"Not really, but again, I do appreciate you telling me, even if it's hard to hear," she answered.

"What am I going to do, Jillian? The woman brings out the absolute worst in me. When I try being nice to her, she comes after me. If I'm not, she makes sleazy comments in front of others. And the gossip magazines...they make me sick. "

"I wish I had an answer for you, honey. The Internet suggests she is having marital problems, and one of her sons is also making the news in negative ways, but who knows if any of that is true?"

"Even if it is, it doesn't mean she has to make my life miserable, just because hers is."

"I know, it shouldn't." She hesitated. "Maybe she wishes she hadn't made such a big mistake and let you go years ago. I know I'd be pretty upset if I'd made that big of a blunder. Maybe she wants you back," Jillian said.

"Well, she can't have me. I'm completely and utterly taken," he told her, putting his hands on her shoulders.

"I'm really glad to hear that," Jillian said, hugging John tightly, like she was afraid to let go of him. As she held him, she said a silent prayer that the fear she was feeling would not rule her heart.

The paparazzi wasn't getting bad for just John. After they figured out Jillian and John's relationship, some photographers started hanging around at some of the book signings. One magazine had a shot of her reading from her book. It talked about how Jillian had started the blog and book because of her broken heart over John and Monica! Never mind that John and Monica hadn't even seen each other during any of the time the blog had begun or the book was written, or that John and Jillian were not together as a couple either at that point, but that was the way "Hollywood" worked. The only good thing about it was that it sold a lot of books, although Jillian preferred not to sell them for that reason.

Everywhere she and John went, there seemed to be more people noticing them and snapping photos. They were even followed home a few times by the photographers, leading them to consider fencing in the entire property for the very first time. Jillian hated the idea of the front yard being gated, but then again, these people seemed to have no morals or limits, and she worried not only about their privacy, but their safety. She also knew that after the movie John was working on hit the theaters, it would be even worse. She guessed it was a part of the price one paid for success, unfortunately. They reluctantly called a few companies to come in and give them estimates on the project.

There were several bright spots during this otherwise hectic and stressful time. The first one was that John had hired someone—actually a team of people—to put a massive number of LED Christmas lights on the house. He also had a beautiful, large fresh-cut Christmas tree delivered, which they centered before the tall windows of the library. It took them two nights and a very tall stepladder to decorate the tree, with many boxes of brand new ornaments they had picked out together the evening the tree arrived. John also put lights and evergreen garland on the staircase railing and around the foyer. It was quite an impressive and festive display, and an even more delightful surprise.

The Christmas before, there had not been one decoration in the house. Jillian had left a small artificial tree for John on Christmas Eve, which this year he put in the center of the dining room table. She had also given him a snow globe, which he placed in a prominent place on the book table in the library, where he could see it every day. He declared it his favorite decoration of all. Seeing it made Jillian excited at the thought of him opening up the box with the family crèche in it this year. It had been safely delivered, as the snow globe had been the year before, to Karen's house. Jillian could hardly wait.

Another highlight was a call out of the blue from Meredith, the young woman Jillian used to see while out on her bike rides in the neighborhood. Meredith, her husband, and their son, Charlie, had recently moved to another neighborhood, and had pretty much started over. One of the best new things they had incorporated into their lives was belonging to a church, something Meredith had never considered until she met Jillian.

Meredith sounded excited as she talked about Charlie, her husband, the new house and neighborhood, and the Bible study she so enjoyed at church.

"Well, now to the real reasons I'm calling. First, may I use you as a personal reference? I'm hoping to work part-time at our church's daycare and preschool as an aide," Meredith said proudly.

"That's wonderful, Meredith. You'll be a real gift to them," Jillian replied

"Thanks, Jillian. And one of the best things is that they let the workers' children come along with their parents. And Jillian—Charlie's going to be a big brother!" the young woman pronounced excitedly.

"That's the best news yet, Meredith," she said. Jillian gave her her contact information and told Meredith she could call her anytime.

After they hung up, Jillian just smiled. God was at it again—another—no, three other—new creations—Meredith, her new job, and her new baby.

But the best and brightest spot during the Advent season was the arrival of Marty, who came home from Senegal for good after a two-year internship. John was filming when her plane landed on Friday afternoon, but Jillian was free to pick her up.

Jillian couldn't believe how good Marty looked for someone who had been deathly ill just two months before. The situation had been one of the most horrifying in Jillian's life, when Marty's boyfriend and colleague, Michael, had called to tell her that Marty had been put into isolation with a high fever. When one's daughter is working on Ebola research, that isn't what one wants to hear. It turned out to be Dengue fever, a serious but less deadly mosquito-borne disease.

So despite being a few pounds lighter and her hair a bit thinner, Jillian thought Marty seemed even prettier and happier than she had been when they visited her in Senegal months earlier. She was certain that the thought of being at the same school with Michael for a semester had something to do with the radiance coming from her daughter. Jillian could now actually claim to understand how special it was to be in love with someone, and to be loved back. She was very happy for her daughter to have found that same kind of love. Almost as happy as she was to have her—*finally*—home!

The route home from the airport had never seemed shorter than it did that day, as Jillian and Marty talked nonstop the entire way. It was almost the shortest day of the year, so it was already getting dark when they arrived at the house. The Christmas lights had come on automatically and were all ablaze when they drove up the circle drive.

"Wow!" said Marty. "It's amazing, Mom!"

"John had it done for me. Last year there wasn't one decoration in this house, and now it's practically a showcase," she said. Then she told Marty about the special gift that she was giving John.

"That makes me want to cry just hearing about it, Mom. Now I can't wait for Christmas Day to see Dad open it, too!"

Now it was Jillian's turn to feel like crying, just hearing her daughter calling someone "Dad."

They pulled the luggage out of the car and onto the floor of the garage. They dragged a heavy, bulging duffle into the house, leaving the one with non-essentials in the garage until Marty left to go to Stanford in a few weeks. There was no sense unpacking it when it had to be moved again. Plus, it was even heavier than its predecessor, so they thought better of moving it more than necessary.

They settled Marty into her room, then sat in the breakfast nook sharing some cocoa, stories, and laughter. One doesn't always appreciate little things like that, unless it is months between them. Jillian couldn't seem to stop smiling as she sat back and listened to her glowing daughter.

Sunday was Nancy and Buck's wedding during church. John, Jillian, and Marty arrived in time to have a piece of wedding cake and coffee, which Nancy and Buck had provided during the fellowship hour between services. The two looked radiant. Buck was in white from hat to toe, with the exception of a bolo tie with a beautiful blue stone in the center. Nancy wore a pretty blue dress, which accented her eyes and was the "color of Advent," she said.

Jillian, John, and Marty were introduced to the rest of Nancy's family. They knew one grandson from their own wedding, when he served as their photographer. He was at it again, camera at the ready, taking shots as they enjoyed the cake. After the service, they were all going to celebrate with a brunch. When Nancy found out that Marty would be in town, she invited her along as well.

"What's one more?" Nancy had remarked. Jillian thought she had a point, as Nancy had six children, their six spouses, and nineteen grandchildren who were all in attendance. With Marty, there would be thirty-six of them—"a nice even number" as Nancy put it.

Having the wedding vows during the worship service was very moving for everyone in attendance. The church was packed and decorated for the Advent season. Pastor Jim talked about the hope and anticipation of the season, and tied it in nicely to the beginning of a marriage. John slipped his hand into Jillian's during the ceremony, remembering their own special day in this very sanctuary, and the hope and anticipation they had felt. So far, their life together had been everything they had hoped for, and more.

Some of Nancy's children and grandchildren sang a special song for them after the vows, then the service continued as usual. It was a church service many would speak about for years to come, and a great witness of what a Christian marriage was about—love,

Kathy J. Jacobson

commitment, and faith. Nancy and Buck seemed so happy, and it put everyone in a festive mood and ready to celebrate Christmas.

The next day, while John was working, Jillian and Marty did some last-minute shopping, then had lunch together downtown. The two had missed their mother-daughter outings over the past two years, and were ready to make up for lost time.

Once they returned home, after a final stop at the supermarket, they embarked on phase one of a baking marathon. Mother and daughter were making all of their favorite Christmas cookie recipes. They made a list of cookie varieties and another list of recipients. Their operation would continue into the next day, as both lists were extensive. They smiled and sang Christmas songs as they worked together, relishing each moment. It had been years since they had shared such a special time together.

The days passed quickly, and Christmas Eve came before they knew it. John had that day through New Year's Day off, and he seemed ecstatic to be home and away from the set—and especially away from Monica. John had said that the past week was a bit more tolerable. Perhaps the holidays were helping to bring Monica and her family back together, they both thought. Or it could be that he didn't have as many romantic scenes with her either that week. Unfortunately, the most intimate one was still to come, and John was not cherishing the thought. And Jillian definitely wasn't either.

After the holiday break, there were only bits and pieces to finish for the movie in Los Angeles. Then on the twelfth of January, the entire cast and crew were heading to Alaska for two weeks of on-location filming in the snow and cold. Carson Stone demanded authenticity in his films. That was part of the reason he was up for an Academy Award almost every year, although he still had yet to bring home a statue.

During the day, Jillian, Marty, and John worked on making the recipe of fish stew that Maria had sent them. It was another one of John's mother's recipes, and the family always had it every Christmas Eve. And of course, Jillian made John's mother's cannoli like last year, praying it would turn out as well again. Thankfully, it was a success once more.

There were several times during the day when Jillian's eyes began to fill with tears of joy. She had always dreamed about what it would be like to be home during the holidays with a husband and her daughter—as a family—and now the dream had come true. Several times throughout the day, she caught John watching her, seeming to read her mind. He looked like he might be having similar thoughts running through his own mind, as his jaw spread into that precious grin and his eyes seemed to have a special twinkle in them. This was John's first Christmas as a spouse and a father. It was an extra special holiday, indeed.

They had invited Karen, Robert, and Rick to join them that evening. They were coming for fish stew and some Christmas pancakes for Rick, around seven. Jillian had also invited them to attend church with them at eleven, certain that Karen would never go for that idea. But Karen had pleasantly surprised her by accepting the invitation.

Jillian was going to play her guitar with several others at the service. She had been happy to practice for it at home, finding it a relaxing exercise during these hectic past few weeks. They had had two rehearsals together at church, and felt they were ready for the night.

After dinner, they all enjoyed the cannoli, even Rick. He thought it was almost as good as the pancakes, in which Jillian had put miniature red- and green-colored chocolate candies for the occasion.

They relaxed in the living room afterward, a fire burning in the fireplace. It was cooler than last Christmas, so there was no guitar playing outside this time, but John had asked Jillian to play and sing "Silent Night," like she had the year before out near the pool. She hadn't known that night that he was standing on his deck overlooking the backyard, watching and listening. The song on the guitar would become a Christmas Eve tradition for years to come in their household.

This year it was even better because Marty was there to sing it with Jillian for the first time in a number of years. Jillian sang the first verse, Marty the second, and then on the final one, Marty sang a descant that Jillian had learned at church as a child and later taught her daughter. They had sung it together in Tanzania and on occasion at their church in Madison for Christmas Eve worship. It had been a long time since they had done it together, but some things one never forgets.

After "Silent Night," Jillian said she wanted to sing one more song, and began to pick and sing "Ave Maria," John's favorite Christmas song since childhood. John was very moved that she had learned it just for him.

Following the music, John brought out a large, brightly wrapped package for Rick. In it was a youth-sized Northwestern football and a Northwestern football jersey with a number "7," John's number, and hopefully his great-nephew John Anthony's number the next season. Above the number was the name "RICK." Jillian had gotten John a similar one with "Romano" on the back for Valentine's Day.

"We know baseball's your game, but we hope you like them," John said, then explained the significance of the number.

Rick was ecstatic and asked if he could wear the jersey to

church. Karen looked at Jillian for an answer, not knowing how formal things would be. Rick had a tie along in case he needed one with his new white dress shirt he was wearing.

"Of course," Jillian said, "if it's okay with Karen and Robert."

"Mama Karen, Papa Roberto, is it okay?"

They both nodded, enjoying Rick's enthusiasm. Jillian saw Karen's eyes light up when Rick used the words Mama and Papa. She was pretty sure that they hoped that they might be Rick's real mama and papa one day.

"It's pretty cold. Why don't you wear it over your shirt? The purple would look nice over that white," Karen said.

John piped in, "Yes, that would look like the long-sleeved undershirts quarterbacks often wear under our jerseys."

With John's endorsement, Rick was okay with that plan.

It was time to go to church. Everyone, and the guitar, squeezed into John's Land Rover. On the way to church, they sang along to Christmas songs on the radio. Even Rick started to sing one, and Jillian thought he had a very pleasant voice. Maybe she could teach him how to play the guitar and see if he would try singing more. Music was so therapeutic, and she thought it might be beneficial to him.

The service seemed extra-special to Jillian that night. She was quite certain that was due to the fact that she was standing between her husband and her daughter, another "first" in her Christmas Eve experiences. She had never felt so truly blessed in her entire life.

At the end of the service, she played "Silent Night" with the other guitarists as the lights were dimmed and candles were lighted. She looked at her family and her friends in the pew. It was an amazing sight. Marty was home from Senegal. Her friends, who hadn't been in a church in years, were singing along with a boy whom they needed almost as much as he needed them. And then there was John, who was looking straight at her and smiling as he sang.

The candlelight glowing on their faces made the entire scene ethereal. As Jillian strummed the final chords, she knew that she had never felt God's presence so deeply or clearly as on this special Christmas Eve. She thought about how Emmanuel means "God with us." *God certainly is,* Jillian thought.

Jillian felt like a child on Christmas morning. She quietly hopped out of bed, trying not to disturb her exhausted husband, and headed for the kitchen. She took a pan of pecan rolls, Marty's favorite, out of the refrigerator to rise before baking. She brought out the French press and began to make coffee. There was fresh-squeezed orange juice in the refrigerator. She cut up some fresh fruit, arranging it on a Christmas platter she had bought for the occasion. That would round out their breakfast. She put the rolls into the oven, and as she turned on the timer, she felt two warm, strong arms wrap around her waist.

"Merry Christmas, Mrs. Romano," John spoke softly into her ear.

Jillian turned around to face John. She was always amazed how much more she loved him each and every day, but on this day, the feeling was so overwhelming that she was almost beside herself.

"Merry Christmas, Mr. Romano," she said, in an equally soft tone.

John was about to kiss Jillian when Marty walked into the room, wrapped in a robe made of Senegalese fabric.

"Don't stop on my account, Dad," she said with an impish smile.

"Okay, I won't," he answered, and gave Jillian a huge kiss.

Jillian always felt like they were the only two people in the world whenever he kissed her like that. They reluctantly separated, and John looked lovingly into her eyes.

"Hold that thought," Jillian mouthed to him.

He smiled and nodded.

The three ate together in the breakfast nook. Even though she adored the pecan rolls almost as much as Marty did, Jillian could hardly eat. She was so excited about the gift for John, which they would be opening as soon as they were finished, that it was all she could think about. After the present opening, they would get ready to go down to St. Anthony's and serve at the free community Christmas dinner, as she and John had done the year before. His appearance at the dinner had been unexpected, and that he came to help had been beyond her wildest dreams.

Like a well-practiced team, the three of them cleared the dishes from the table, wiped the countertops, and went into the library to get to the business of opening gifts. The furniture had been rearranged in the room the past few weeks so that the love seat and several comfortable chairs were situated for appropriate tree-gazing. John and Jillian occupied the love seat, while Marty claimed a comfy, overstuffed chair that she pronounced as hers for the duration of her stay.

They gave Marty a gift of a new smartphone, something she had wanted badly, as hers was "ancient," according to her, and she had no money to replace it. They also gave her a necklace they had bought for her in Rome. It had been difficult not to give it to her when they had visited her in Senegal, but now they were happy that they had waited. According to the man who made it, it was a "daughter" necklace.

Jillian opened a gift from Marty, a beautiful little coffee set, coffee beans, and the spices needed to make what had been her favorite hot drink in Senegal, Cafe Touba. Then it was John's turn for a gift from Marty. They laughed as John held up a pair of brightly colored, Senegalese motif "party pants."

"I just had to get you those, but here is your real gift," Marty said, handing him another package.

John opened the brightly wrapped package and held up a beautiful Senegalese wood carving of a man, a woman, and a girl in the center. They were holding hands.

"I know I'm not a kid anymore, and even a little taller than Mom now, but when I was a girl and we would go to the carver's row in Arusha, I always wished I had both a mom and a dad, and could get one of the carvings like this. So now that I do, I had this made. Thanks for making my dream a reality—Dad," she said.

John was speechless, as was Jillian. Suddenly Jillian's gift to John seemed second place, but that was okay with her. The happiness exuding from her daughter, and the honored look on her husband's face, were beyond anything for which she could have ever hoped.

John cleared his throat to try to speak, as Marty came over toward the love seat. He stood up, and they hugged each other, then Marty motioned for Jillian to join them. That did it for Jillian, and tears began to flow as they shared a group hug.

After they all composed themselves, John said to Marty, "Well, you're a hard act to follow," as he pulled a small box from under the tree and handed it to Jillian.

"John, I assumed that all these beautiful decorations were my Christmas gift," she said.

"Just part of it. I had to give you a little something," he told her, as Jillian began to unwrap the box.

"It was designed especially for you by Ken down at the jewelry store," he said.

Jillian opened the velvet box which held a platinum ring, with a very unique design, but it was clearly a key.

"It's one of a kind. It's the key to my heart—and only you have it," he said.

Jillian had just gotten herself under control, and now this. John obviously must have sensed her trepidation over the past month during the movie filming and was making a real statement with this beautiful ring, which she put on the ring finger of her right hand.

She couldn't speak, just looked into his eyes, then pulled him into a tight hug. They parted and then just looked at each other for a long moment.

"Okay, you two," Marty finally said. "There's still one box left under the tree."

The reminder helped Jillian come back to this world, and her heart leapt. John sat back down on the love seat as Jillian carefully carried the large box and placed it gingerly on the floor in front of him.

Jillian had purposely made it easy for him to open the box, so it wouldn't have to be jostled about. He pulled off the decorated top of the outer box. There was a self-stick note attached to the top of the plain brown box inside, the one it had been stored in for years inside the large trunk.

*Merry Christmas, John
With much love from Jillian (and Tommy)*

Jillian could tell that the "and Tommy" part was confusing John, but he continued to open the flaps of the box. He pulled out the protective paper and just stared.

"It looks just like…"

"It *is*," Jillian interjected.

It took another moment for that to sink in. Then John put his hand to his mouth to stifle a cry. Tears welled in his eyes, and he grasped for Jillian's hand with his other hand.

After a moment he finally spoke a single word. *"Where?"*

Jillian told him the story about the neighbor calling Tommy a few days before Thanksgiving, and Tommy going over to get the trunk and boxes from the man's garage in Belvidere. When he opened the trunk, Tommy had been treated to this wonderful and unexpected discovery. He had said it was like finding treasure.

John was finally regaining his composure. "That's what you two were talking about on the phone, wasn't it?" he asked softly, still very moved.

Jillian nodded her head.

John carefully took the pieces out of the box and assembled the ensemble under the Christmas tree, saving the coveted baby Jesus for last. There had always been a big fight between John and his brother, Anthony, over who got to put Jesus in the manger on Christmas Day. It had become so heated that eventually his parents made the boys draw straws for the honor.

"I think you should do the honor, John," Jillian said. "It's your gift."

He looked at her, another one of those looks that made her feel like they were the only two people in the world. "I think you should do it, Jillian. You're a savior—*my* savior," he said.

Jillian was genuinely touched by his sincere and loving words. "Let's both do it, because you are mine, too," she suggested. Together they carefully placed the smiling figure in his bed of hay, and Jillian felt like their Savior was smiling—for them.

The community dinner seemed even busier than the previous year. They were glad to have an extra, experienced helper with them in Marty. To Jillian's amazement, Drew and Greta were there, too, ready to work the set-up and first serving shift.

"Hi, Jillian," Greta said. "Merry Christmas!"

"Greta! I'm so happy to see you. I didn't know you were going to be here."

"We weren't planning on it. I just heard about this last week when Drew was discussing how he spent his last Christmas Day. I thought it sounded like an awesome idea, so here we are. It just may become our new tradition, like it was with you," she said smiling.

Drew stood next to her, beaming. Jillian could barely believe the new creation he was becoming since he married Greta. The year before, Drew clearly didn't want to work at the dinner, and couldn't wait to bolt out of there when his one-hour serving shift was over.

"Speaking of family, my—*our*—daughter is here!" Jillian exclaimed, and introduced Marty to Drew and Greta. They all hugged each other, then got to work cooking and setting the tables, talking as they did.

Finally the doors "opened for business," and a long line of people of every age, size, gender, and race filed in. Among the first people in line were Karen, Robert, and Rick—another great surprise.

"I was going to make a huge dinner when Rick said he wanted to come here, like he always did on Christmas Day. We couldn't say no to that. And when we are done eating, we would be happy to help out in any way that we can," Karen said, a huge smile on her face.

Rick looked exuberant. He was wearing his new football jersey, and Jillian wondered if he would ever take it off.

John was ladling gravy again, claiming that he was now an expert. Marty was in charge of the mashed potatoes next to him, and Jillian scooped corn. Before they knew it, an hour had flown by.

Karen, Rick, and Robert had finished their dinners and asked if they could relieve them so they could eat. They decided that that was a wonderful idea, and it would allow them to get home a little earlier than they had planned. John couldn't wait to make a call to Tommy. Knowing the Romano family was busy working on this day with Maria's business, they had suggested a time frame from late afternoon to early evening to contact them.

The food tasted wonderful. There was something sacred about sharing a dinner with people one didn't even know, yet who seemed like friends. Jillian always thought that it was the way God intended the world to operate—like everyone was just one huge family.

John, Jillian, and Marty cleared their plates. There were no dramatic tray droppings this year, and no one shouting and cursing at a little boy. Instead, Rick stood between his foster parents proudly ladling gravy. He had demanded to have the same job that John had been doing, an indication of how much Rick looked up to him.

The day was very special. However, little did they know, that while they were eating, their picture had been taken. They didn't discover it until the next week when it appeared on a magazine cover, with a caption under it wondering if the family had fallen on hard times. Jillian just shook her head in disbelief when she read that. The press seemed to have no shame in what they printed.

It wasn't as bad as other recent photos, however. They just wouldn't leave the John and Monica theme alone, and there was photo after photo in magazines and online. It was clear that somehow the paparazzi was getting onto the movie lot and taking photos during the filming. Jillian wondered if they had some kind of "spy" on the crew to get those kind of photos.

John, Jillian, and Marty took their serving positions back, as Robert, Rick, and Karen were heading home. Rick and Robert planned to throw the football in the backyard for a while, then play basketball. Rick had gotten a basketball and a portable, adjustable basketball hoop for Christmas, along with a Lakers jersey.

"Come over soon, so I can show you my presents," Rick told John and Jillian. "And don't forget you're going to teach me how to throw a spiral," he said directly to John.

"Of course. The next time I come over," John replied.

"Merry Christmas!" Rick said to them, beaming a huge, bright smile.

"Feliz Navidad!" Robert interjected, and Rick smiled at him.

"I'm teaching him Spanish," Rick said proudly.

"Merry Christmas and Feliz Navidad to all of you, too," Jillian replied. She watched the family exit, Robert's arm lovingly wrapped around Rick's shoulders. Last year, Rick had been pushed and shoved out of the room by an irate parent. Jillian thought again. What a difference—what a new creation.

They arrived home at four o'clock their time and called Tommy. They had decided on a video call, so everyone could see one another, and so Tommy could see the crèche assembled under the tree, just as his grandparents, and later his parents, had done.

At one point, pretty much the entire family on both ends was in tears. At least they were tears of joy, as John scanned his computer's camera over the manger scene which sat serenely beneath the massive tree.

After the manger viewing, John and Jillian took the computer back to the kitchen and put it on the counter, as it was easier to see, and be seen, that way.

Jillian couldn't believe how handsome—and big and strong—John Anthony had gotten. Obviously, the football diet, weight room, and practice with the team had paid off. She noticed him staring into the video screen, looking a slight bit to the side, where Marty was standing, she presumed. The poor guy. She didn't have the heart to mention Michael in her conversations with the younger Romanos. She hoped that soon John Anthony would find someone of his own. She was certain there were many beautiful and nice young women at Northwestern.

Kathy J. Jacobson

They talked about what a busy two days it had been for Tommy's family. They had worked all day long on Christmas Eve, then gone to Midnight Mass, and had to be up at 4:00 a.m. Christmas morning to bake for their home orders. Some of the main dishes had been made the day before, but they had had many orders on Christmas Eve, too, for the fish stew and other traditional offerings.

They were happy that they were taking the next few days off before beginning preparations for New Year's Eve and Day. There weren't quite as many preorders for those holidays, but they would be open all day on both days. Many people had ordered ahead on pizzas, and they knew even more might stop by at the last minute or call for a carryout order. Pizza was not something Maria had originally planned on offering, but she had tweaked some recipes into some that she thought were good enough to put her name on, and her customers loved them. John told Maria that the long days were the price one paid for doing something very well, which made her smile.

They talked a few more minutes, then regretfully said good night. Tommy's family needed to relax and then get some much deserved sleep after the grind of the past week, and especially the last two days.

Just as the call ended, the doorbell rang. They all looked at one another. The first thing that ran through Jillian's mind was paparazzi. She wondered if they would truly be that ridiculous.

"I'll get it," John said, and jumped to his feet from the stool he was sitting on in the kitchen.

A moment later, he returned to the room. "Marty—there's a special delivery for you in the foyer," he said, a sparkle in his eyes.

Seconds later, they heard a scream of delight coming from the front of the house.

"What in the world?" Jillian asked.

John just smiled. It was quiet a moment, then they heard laughter and voices, and footsteps heading their way.

Marty and Michael appeared in the kitchen, their smiles as wide as a mile.

Michael went over and hugged Jillian and wished her a Merry Christmas. Marty went over to John and threw her arms around him.

"Thank you, Dad! Michael says you arranged this," she said in a highly emotional state.

"I know what it feels like to have someone special in your life," he said, and threw a glance Jillian's way.

Jillian's heart was almost as full as her daughter's, especially after that comment. They all sat down in the breakfast nook to talk, Marty and Michael squished together like sardines. John put his arm around Jillian and pulled her tight against his side.

They talked and laughed for hours, until they all found their stomachs making noises. John said he had a surprise for them and pulled pizzas from Leo's restaurant out of the freezer. "They're not as good as they are fresh, but they will do," he said.

Jillian took out some greens and vegetables and made a quick salad, and soon they were sitting down to eat. John said the table prayer, thanking God for the newborn Savior, for food, for family, and for friends who were like family. Then they all heartily dug in. Leo's pizzas—even frozen—were amazing, and there was little in the way of leftovers.

Cleanup was simple. Jillian suggested that Marty show Michael to one of the guest rooms, then they could "have" the library, as long as they remembered to turn out all those Christmas lights when they went up for the night. Jillian was pretty sure that Marty and Michael would appreciate some alone time, and quite frankly, she was pretty sure she and John would, too.

Chapter Eleven

Everyone slept late the next morning, which was a refreshing
change, especially for John. Marty and Michael also had had
little time off the past few months, working many long days, nights,
and on-call hours. Each of them was looking forward to a change
of pace. The only one who wouldn't really have one was Jillian.
She would be right back on the bookstore circuit that weekend. At
least she had one full day with her family before that happened.
They had absolutely nothing planned for the day after Christmas,
and it was a glorious feeling.

Jillian threw a load of laundry into the washer, and then fed
and brushed Lucy, the orange-haired cat. She had been in hiding
the past few days with all the strangers in the house. She had met
and liked Marty, but for years, it was just she and John in the big
house, until Jillian came along. Lucy wasn't used to so many new
people invading her turf all at once, so she spent most of the holidays in the huge laundry room on her fluffy bed, or in the wide
window sill laying in the sun.

Jillian made some coffee, poured two mugs, and went to find
John. Marty and Michael were out for a walk. She found him in

their favorite room, the library. She watched from the doorway. He was sitting on the love seat, just staring at the crèche under the tree.

She almost hated to disturb him, but after a minute, she quietly entered the room. "Hi," she said softly. "Mind if I join you?"

"I'd love it if you would join me," he said, holding out his hand to her.

She set the coffee down on the table next to the love seat, took his hand, and sat down. She could never seem to get close enough to John. Even when they were touching, it seemed too far away. He kissed her forehead tenderly.

"A penny for your thoughts," she said.

He let out a small sigh. "I was thinking about my brother." John's brother, Anthony, had died almost eleven years ago from Alzheimer's disease. It had been a very early onset and had been very hard on the family, especially Anthony's son—John's nephew—Tommy.

"I thought that maybe he had thrown it out or given the crèche away. And now I find out that he helped save it by having it stored at his neighbor's. I think he knew that he was getting worse and wanted it kept safe. The only problem was that he couldn't remember to tell Tommy what he had done with it. We all thought that it was lost forever."

Jillian was silent. She just let John talk, holding his hand. He had had a tenuous relationship with his brother his entire life, which he seemed to be starting to work through, even though Anthony was gone.

He looked at the manger scene again. "We used to fight so much over that baby Jesus. I wish we could have done what you and I did yesterday—we could have put him in the manger *together*."

"Most of us wish that we could have 'do-overs,' John," Jillian finally said. "Maybe that's what heaven will be like—one big do-over."

Kathy J. Jacobson

"Maybe," he said, and pulled her close. "You always make things seem more hopeful, Jillian, like somehow even the worst things in life can be worked out."

"You're giving me too much credit, John. It's not me. New creation, remember?"

"New creation," he said softly, enfolding her in his arms.

John showed Marty and Michael around Los Angeles while Jillian was signing books, then dropped them off in the afternoon at one of the bookstores. They surprised Jillian as they both came through the line, bringing a copy of her book up for her to sign. They could get away with it—at least at this point—as no one knew that they were related to her or John. She just laughed and played along with it, like they were any other customers. The only difference were her words to Marty as she left the signing table.

"See you later, honey," she whispered.

"Thank you, ma'am," Marty said, smiling as she and Michael walked out arm in arm.

When the signing was over, John picked Jillian up at a back door, and then they were all off to dinner. They let Marty and Michael choose the type of food. They wanted Mexican, as they hadn't had it in ages, they said. John and Jillian looked at each other and said in unison, "Paco's Tacos!"

Paco's, again, did not disappoint. It was the best place for tacos and other authentic dishes in town—at least they thought so. Pete had introduced Jillian to the place shortly after they met. While they ate, Jillian told them how Pete had brought her to this place, then gave the latest update on the twins.

Gus and Grace were doing better than expected and might come home a couple of weeks early. In the meantime, Jillian and Marty made a plan to go and see the babies on Monday afternoon. Marty had heard so much about them that she just had to see them, and better yet, hold them. She also wanted to go late enough in the afternoon so that she might be able to meet Pete, a person she felt like she already knew.

On Monday, Marty hit the jackpot at the NICU, holding and feeding both babies and meeting Pete. They had unfortunately missed Kelly by half an hour, but Jillian hoped they might have another opportunity while Marty was still in town.

"I'd know who you were any day," Pete said the moment he saw Marty, then picked her up and hugged her with his huge arms. He set her back down gently. "Marty. You look a lot like your Mom."

Jillian was thrilled any time someone said something like that. Not only was it a huge compliment, but growing up as an adopted child, there was never anyone whom she truly resembled. Occasionally, someone would say that she looked like her mother, and her Mom would beam. She now understood that proud feeling. While she had liked it when people had said that about her and her mom, deep down she knew that it was only a coincidence. Now, with Marty, her only blood relative, she cherished the comment.

"And I'd know who you were any day, too, Pete. My mom described you to a T," she said.

"Did she now?" Pete asked in a teasing manner.

"Okay, let's go see the little ones," Jillian said, changing the subject, and turning to go into the NICU.

They scrubbed and sat down in some rockers, taking turns holding and feeding Gus and Grace. Compared to when they were born, and to many of the new arrivals in the nursery, the twins were starting to seem big to Pete and Jillian. Their skin was changing, becoming less translucent and more the creamy, rosy color of a newborn. Gus was still on a bit of oxygen, but they were optimistic that he would not need it much longer, and planned to begin weaning him off it shortly.

"Pete, they are really beautiful babies," Marty said after she had held each of them, and she and Pete gently put them back down to sleep, their stomachs full.

"They take after their mother," he said with love in his voice and eyes. Jillian thought that she and Kelly were two of the luckiest women, having two incredible men like John and Pete love them both so dearly. She reminded herself to never take that for granted.

"I look forward to meeting her," Marty told him.

"I know she'll want to meet you, too. Unfortunately, her office called her with a problem that needed solving in person, and she was the only one who knew what to do. She's really smart, too," he said sincerely, and with pride.

"Another time," Marty said.

"Yes, another time. Thanks for coming, both of you," he said, and gave them hugs.

"Just think, Pete, it won't be long and they will be home," Jillian said.

"It's hard to believe—and I have to say, a little scary," he said.

"It's always a little scary bringing home a new baby, but you and Kelly will be great," Jillian replied.

"Yes, I concur. I can tell that you are an awesome dad, Pete," Marty said.

Pete actually blushed, and gave them both another hug. "You guys are the best."

Marty and Jillian stepped into the hospital elevator. The door closed, and Marty let out a little whistle. "Wow, you weren't exaggerating about Pete at all, Mom. He's both gorgeous and sweet."

"Yes, he is both of those things," she admitted.

"It must have been a tough decision to turn him down," she said.

"Not really. His heart was already taken, and so was mine—I just didn't really want to admit it." She paused. "Do you think I made the wrong choice?" Jillian asked.

"I think Pete is mad about Kelly. I think Dad is mad about you. And Dad is pretty gorgeous and sweet, too—for a dad," she said, smiling. "Seems like the right decision to me, Mom."

"Me, too," Jillian replied, with absolutely no doubt in her heart or mind about that.

New Year's Eve snuck up on them. Marty and Michael had been researching fun things to do that night. Jillian told them that they should go out, but she and John were going to stay in this time. More and more people were recognizing John, and huge crowds of people were not a good idea in their case.

Marty and Michael found some options they thought sounded interesting, but they were both pretty broke. When Marty said something to that effect, John looked at Jillian. She smiled and gave him a "go ahead" nod.

"Well, I'm not broke," he said. "So, what are you looking at?"

Marty showed him the computer screen. She had pulled up information for the fireworks celebration on the Catalina Yacht at Long Beach.

"So, let's see. This is your first choice?"

Marty nodded. John's fingers pecked at the computer keyboard, and he got his credit card out of his wallet. He punched in the numbers. "Does this look right? I don't want to hit 'submit' unless you approve," he said.

Marty looked at the screen. "Dad, that's too much," she said. "We don't have to have the best seats on the boat."

"Why not?"

"They're too expensive."

"They are expensive, but I've never had to pay for a prom or anything else like that. It would make me happy to do this for you and Michael tonight."

"Are you sure?"

"Positive."

"Okay, if you're sure, go ahead and hit the button, Dad. Thank you so much!"

Marty took over the keyboard and had the tickets sent to her phone, then looked at John.

"For someone who's new at it, you're pretty good at this dad stuff," Marty said with a happy smile.

"That's one of the nicest things I've ever been told," John said sincerely to Marty, then looked at Jillian, who was loving every moment of the exchange.

Marty jumped up and hugged John, then ran off to tell Michael, who was reading a book in the library, that their plans for the evening were set. He was an avid reader and had fallen in love with the room, the same way Jillian had the first time she saw it. They heard a loud "yes!" all the way in the kitchen.

That made them both smile. Jillian got up from the chair and walked up to John, who was still glowing from his daughter's compliment.

"So, what are *we* going to do tonight, Mrs. Romano?" John asked, putting his hands on her waist.

Jillian answered him simply with a kiss.

"I can live with that," he said, and kissed her back.

John made dinner for Jillian that night. He felt so bad for being gone so much lately, and the next day was his last day off until the filming was completed.

They ate by candlelight in the dining room, next to one another at one end of the table, as was their custom when they ate at the huge table. Tonight's fare was a portabella and pasta dish, with salad and a crusty-on-the-outside, soft-on-the-inside baguette that John actually made from scratch, using one of his mom's recipes that Maria had recently sent.

They would be calling Tommy late tomorrow night. The last they had heard, Maria's business had gained such a good reputation that she actually had to turn away some customers. This turned out to be one of her biggest weekends, between parties for the New Year and for football games on New Year's Day. It sounded like she was going to have to expand her space and hire some more employees as soon as possible.

They cleared the dishes. Jillian was just about to turn off her cell phone for a while, wanting some uninterrupted time with her husband, when Carol's number flashed across the screen.

"Hi, Carol!" Jillian said, excited to hear from her best friend from Wisconsin.

"My dear Jillian, how are you?" Carol asked as John came up behind Jillian and put his arms around her, putting his chin on her unoccupied shoulder. It sounded noisy in the background as Carol spoke.

John began to nuzzle her neck as she answered Carol. "Oh, I'm doing well—very well, in fact," she said, as John kissed her neck. "Is it cold there?"

"Not really," Carol said.

"Really?"

"Is it cold there?" Carol asked.

"Not at all," she said as John kissed her unoccupied ear. "I thought Madison was supposed to be in the negatives tonight."

"It might be, but I'm not in Madison," Carol said.

"Where *are* you?" Jillian asked, trying hard to concentrate on her conversation.

"In Las Vegas, with Jerry. We're spending the New Year here," she said.

Jillian was a bit surprised. She had never known Carol to spend a night with someone before, not even with her former boyfriend of many years, Joe.

"Really?" was the best Jillian could offer.

"You sound surprised," Carol said.

"Well, I've known you many years, Carol. I've just never known you to go off to Vegas, or anywhere, with a man before," she replied honestly.

"He's not just a man, Jillian. He's my husband!" Carol exclaimed. "We got married tonight!"

Jillian almost dropped the phone, for more reasons than one. She turned around in John's arms. "Carol and Jerry just got married!"

He stopped kissing her for a moment. "That's great! Congratulations, Carol," he said toward the phone. "Great decision." He continued to kiss Jillian as she tried to talk to her friend.

"I'll call tomorrow and give you the details," Carol said. "It's a little crazy here right now."

Jillian almost told her it was a little crazy where she was, too, but instead replied, "That sounds great. Congratulations again, Carol. I'm so very happy for you."

"I'm happy for me, too, and I'm so happy for you, too, Jillian. We're two lucky ducks. 'Bye, now," Carol said and hung up the phone.

"You're right about that," Jillian said to herself, then met her husband's waiting lips.

Carol called the next day. John and Jillian were watching bits and pieces of football games in the theater room, but neither of their school teams were playing that day, so it wasn't quite as enthralling as the year before. Jillian thought back on that New Year's Day. It was one of the most memorable days in both her and John's lives.

Last year, after having watched Northwestern in a bowl game, enjoying Leo's pizza freshly delivered, and cheering the team to a victory, they had planned to meet in the kitchen and take a walk. When John showed up, a few minutes late, he had handed her a note telling her to call 9-1-1, then collapsed. The next few hours were some of the scariest of Jillian's life, as she had realized for the first time how much John had come to mean to her and that she could not bear the possibility of losing him. Luckily, she didn't have to face that situation, as the brain tumor that had caused his medical event was removed the next day by an excellent surgeon who removed it through John's nasal passage.

"So, let's have the story, Carol," Jillian said to her good friend.

"I was just going to come out to California for a week to visit. I had a hotel booked in Stanford and everything. We were going to come down and surprise you and John today—at least that was the original plan. When I landed at the airport, Jerry was there with a small bag of his own. He said he just couldn't wait anymore, and he wanted me to be his wife—*now*! He pulled out a beautiful ring and asked me to marry him. I said 'yes,' to the applause of about a hundred people at the airport, and we hopped on a plane to Las Vegas. The rest, as they say, is history."

"Well, you certainly did manage to surprise John and me—maybe not the way you had originally intended, but you certainly did."

"And that's not all. When I'm done working in the spring, Jerry will be, too. He gave his notice at the end of the semester. That was news even to me," Carol said. "And there's more."

"Wow! Am I going to like the 'more?'" Jillian asked.

"I sure hope so, because we are moving to Los Angeles. Jerry wants to be closer to his sister and Alan, and I want to be closer to you!"

"Carol!" Jillian felt like crying tears of joy. "That's one of the best things I've heard in a long time. I can't wait."

"Neither can I. In fact, we're going to start house-hunting in a couple of days, then I have to get back to Madison, unfortunately. If you have any suggestions, we're open to them. Bev and Alan are going to help us, too. We're going to stay with them when we come down, but we hope we can see you both, too. And I have to get one of those books of yours!" Jillian couldn't wait to give Carol a copy of the book. She had dedicated the book to two people: *For Carol, who taught me how to heal many hearts, and for John—who healed mine.*

Carol and Jillian discussed some possible times to get together. It was going to be tricky. John's work hours were so unpredictable, and she had book signings the next two days and another on Wednesday night at a church. But somehow, they would make it work.

Jillian sat on John's lap, filling him in on the details of the proposal and subsequent wedding, and the news of Jerry and Carol's plan to move to Los Angeles after they both retired.

"Those are a lot of surprises," John said.

"Yes, it seems that New Year's Day brings them on. Two years ago today, I came to this place, and found out that I was working for you. Last year..." she had to stop for a moment, as it still made her heart sink just thinking about it.

John hugged her tight and kissed the top of her head. Jillian's eyes misted as she lifted her head and looked into his eyes. "At least a few good things happened that day...Northwestern won its bowl game," she said, trying to smile and lighten the moment a bit. "And then there was Leo's pizza. And..." She stopped speaking, overwhelmed with emotion.

John stroked her cheek. "And?" he asked gently.

" And...I found out just how much I loved you," she said, a confession she'd never really made to anyone, not even to John.

"I think we both found that out that day," he said, and kissed her deeply and sweetly.

Just at that moment, Marty and Michael walked into the room.

"What's the score?" Marty asked.

"I have no idea," Jillian said honestly.

"I didn't think so," Marty said, chuckling.

They watched the end of a game together, picking a team to root for based on the fact that Michael had a friend who had graduated from that school. The team won, and they turned off the projector.

"How was the yacht?" Jillian asked.

"We both decided it was the best New Year's Eve we've ever had," Marty said.

"Yes, thank you so much for the tickets," Michael said.

"Were the fireworks good?" John asked.

"They were the best," Michael replied. Marty gave Michael a little look. Jillian thought there were probably more than just fireworks in the sky at midnight. She remembered her and John at Disneyland last winter, and the fireworks bursting in the background just as they kissed, like it was choreographed. John had a dreamy look in his eyes, and she wondered if he was thinking about the same thing.

"What should we do now?" Jillian asked.

"It's a beautiful day. How about something outdoors?" John suggested, knowing that he was going to be inside most of the next two weeks, and then after that, he was off to Alaska.

They decided to go on a bike ride. They put John and Jillian's bikes in the John's Land Rover, then drove to a bike shop that was open 365 days a year, according to the Internet, and rented bikes for Marty and Michael. The shop was located near the entrance to a recreational trail, so they headed out right from the shop and did the twelve-mile loop. It felt great to be outdoors and to get some exercise. With the hectic schedules John and Jillian had had lately, there hadn't been much time for riding.

When they came back, they ordered Chinese food and just kicked back for the rest of the day. John had to be in make-up at five a.m. the next day, so that influenced that decision. Jillian was not looking forward to this final stretch, although it would be exciting to have the film finished. She knew that this was the most special movie John had ever been a part of, and one of the best projects overall of his career. She tried to concentrate on those aspects of the situation, rather than the fact that she wouldn't see much of him the next ten days, and then he would be gone for two full weeks after that. And if she was truthful, she was having trouble shaking the image of a very determined Monica Morgan coming out of John's trailer, which kept invading her mind.

At the end of the night, they called Tommy. Jillian mentally added him as another good thing that had happened on the last New Year's Day. When John had been rushed to the hospital, Tommy hopped on a plane to Los Angeles to be at his uncle's side. Jillian had loved him from the start, and the feeling was mutual. She was so thankful for the special family she had gained through her marriage. It felt like they had been a part of each other's lives from the beginning of time, rather than for just a year.

Tommy sounded tired, but happy. He was so glad that Maria's restaurant, Pasto—which means "meal" in Italian—was doing so well, but he admitted that he was exhausted. He had been recruited into action again that day, as had the entire family. Even John Anthony recorded many of the football games so he could help his mom. That's the type of family they were.

"We are so happy for you both," Jillian said on speaker phone. Maria had already gone to bed, as she had slept a total of two hours in the past twenty-four. Alison was at a friend's house now that her work assignment was over, and John Anthony was fast-forwarding through a bowl game.

"Yes, it's great, although it's almost going too well. We need to expand and get more help as soon as possible. The Main Street program people are thrilled with us and are trying to help us work out the space situation. It would be great if we didn't have to move out completely from our location, but we will see what happens. We have a meeting set up in a week with Pam, the executive director of the program. We are actually closing until next Friday, so Maria can have a few days off. She is very fortunate to have done well enough to do that. Now she has to find another good cook and manager. Maria wants to be able to go to the home football games next fall."

"We hope we can do that sometime, too," John said.

"That would be great, Zio. John Anthony would be ecstatic, especially if he gets to play. He knows there's going to be a good fight for the backup quarterback position, but he thinks he has a reasonable shot at it."

"Tell him to keep that attitude and keep working hard like he has been, and he'll go far," John said.

They talked a minute longer, but Tommy and John both needed to get some sleep.

When John and Jillian walked into the kitchen after the call, Marty and Michael were in a deep discussion. Michael's friend, Tom, had just invited them to come up to his family's "holiday house" in Northern California, next to Mt. Shasta. They had a huge home with many bedrooms and bunks for those who liked to hike in the warm weather or ski in the winter. If Marty and Michael came, it would be Tom's parents, Tom and his girlfriend, and two other students. They had free ski passes for anyone who wanted to ski, and even some equipment. The med students were going to spend a week up there, then head to school and get settled in for the semester.

Jillian and Marty had gone skiing a few times at Cascade Mountain, Devil's Head, and Tyrol Basin in Wisconsin, and twice in the Upper Peninsula of Michigan. It had been fun, but often it was tough to coordinate their schedules, and it was an expensive sport for a single parent, so they didn't get to do it as often as they would have liked.

Jillian could see how torn her daughter was. Marty wanted to be in two places at once. Jillian did what she always tried to do in situations like that—put herself in the other person's shoes. She turned to her daughter and said, "That sounds like a lot of fun. You two should go."

"You think we should?" Marty asked.

"Yes. You haven't been skiing in years, and I hear it is fantastic up there. It would make a special memory for you both," she said.

Michael and Marty looked at each other, trying to make the decision. John looked at Jillian, a kind and supportive expression on his face. Then Marty looked at John. "What do you think, Dad?"

"I think your mom is usually right about these kinds of things. Also, I won't be seeing much of you after today anyway, so it really should be up to the three of you."

"You're sure, Mom?" Marty asked. "You know I can tell if you're not." She said with a wink.

"I'm positive," Jillian said, and smiled at her daughter. She knew her daughter, too, and she knew that she would be disappointed if she didn't go on this ski trip. Her daughter's happiness was just too important to Jillian. She also knew that John was right. He wouldn't see much of them, and on the weekends, neither would Jillian. She also needed to get back to her blog and other notes she was making for her second book. Home wasn't going to be the most exciting place for two twenty-somethings, that was for certain.

Marty came over and hugged her. "I hope I grow up to be just like you someday," her daughter said seriously.

Jillian smiled at her daughter's words, and as always, wondered what she had ever done to deserve such a wonderful gift from God.

Marty and Michael packed up their things later that night, planning to leave early in the morning. They thought they would try to get up when John left, but Jillian was pretty sure that was pure fancy, and she was right. Instead, at seven a.m., she took them to catch the train, which would take them part of the way. Tom would pick them up at a stop, and would then drive them to the house. Jillian was glad someone familiar with the roads would be driving, especially since Marty and Michael hadn't driven on snow and ice in a few years.

Jillian had decided they could deal with the rest of Marty's baggage, which was still in the garage, at a later time. There was nothing in it that was an absolute necessity anyway. It reminded Jillian of Marty's undergraduate years—the coming and the going, the packing and unpacking of college life. She could honestly say she didn't miss that very much.

Even though Marty and Michael didn't make it up in time to see John off, Jillian had gotten up while John was getting ready and made him some coffee and a bagel for him to eat on the way to the studio.

"You spoil me," he said, and kissed her. "I wish I didn't have to go," he added more seriously, pulling her close.

"Me, too," she said.

"Say goodbye to Marty and Michael for me," he said, grabbing the travel mug and paper bag with the bagel, a napkin, and piece of fruit. He started for the door, then turned back and walked up to her. "Oh, and I hope I grow up to be just like you someday, too," he said, and hugged her once more.

The same question from the night before crossed her mind. *What did I ever do to deserve such a wonderful gift from God?*

Chapter Twelve

Jillian could barely believe how much work she got done that day. It helped to have gotten up at 3:45 a.m. The only drawback was the short nap she needed to take after lunch. She wondered how John and the other actors made it through the very long days, yet still managed to look so good on the screen. She supposed the makeup helped, but there is only so much one can do to cover major fatigue.

She was daydreaming about John when her phone rang. It was Carol. She had forgotten that her friend was coming down to house-hunt.

Jillian met Carol and Jerry for lunch, taking them out to celebrate their marriage. She hadn't even gotten them a gift yet, and wondered what they would like or could use. Perhaps they would prefer to give her a suggestion after they found a new home.

The friends conversed for over an hour at lunch, Jerry joining in happily. Jillian could barely believe he was the same sad individual who walked—correction—was dragged into their backyard the previous spring by his sister and Alan, not wanting to be at the wedding reception of people he didn't even know. Actually, at that point in his life, he didn't want to be anywhere, or with anyone, as he was still grieving the loss of his wife. But within a matter of hours, his life, and Carol's life, had been changed—for good. They immediately hit it off, and they hadn't looked back since.

Now the previously unhappy soul was all smiles, had a new hair style, and his beard was neatly trimmed. Jerry had always had a distinguished look, Jillian thought, but now he looked as happy as he did handsome.

The three spent the afternoon driving by some homes they had seen online. They wanted to see the actual house and neighborhoods before they set up an appointment. It was a good idea, as the Internet could make something look great that wasn't, and sometimes worked the opposite way, too.

There were two houses they liked, and called the realtor to see if they could schedule a showing. She told them about an open house the next day that they should consider. They took down the information and drove by. All three of them liked the neighborhood and the yard, and thought it would be worth a look.

Jillian dropped the newlyweds off at their car later that afternoon. John was supposed to be home in an hour, if all had gone well. They were all going to have dinner at Bev and Alan's at seven, so John could relax a bit before dinner, and then get home early for another early morning. Jillian was anxious to hear how the first day back after break had gone. She sincerely hoped things were still on the improvement track.

The six friends had a wonderful evening. Beverly made the best beef brisket Jillian had ever tasted. Bev said she only made it once or twice a year—in the winter when it was cold. It was in the fifties, so Jillian guessed that qualified to the longtime Californians as "cold." She and Carol just laughed, thinking of what the weather was like in Madison. Jillian took out her cell phone and checked the weather "back home." She reported to the group, "The high today was three degrees at three o'clock. The current temperature is zero, and the overnight low is expected to be negative five, with a wind-chill that will make it feel like negative twelve."

"Oh, my goodness! I guess I'd make beef brisket a lot more often if I lived in Wisconsin!" Beverly said. They all laughed, except Bev, who was truly shocked that people really lived in places where it got that cold.

They had a great time, but left just before ten because of John's early call. Jillian drove so John could fall asleep in the car if he so desired. He didn't want to, but he just couldn't help it and was out about two blocks down the street.

Jillian had been glad to hear that the day was fairly pleasant. People came prepared, and he had only one brief scene to do with Monica. He said she didn't say anything to, or about, him today. He thought she actually seemed a bit subdued. Jillian thought that perhaps Monica was finally getting past all her poor behavior. That thought, along with Marty's call before they left for dinner informing them that they had arrived safely at one of the most beautiful places she'd ever seen, had made for an extra enjoyable evening.

The week went by quickly. Bit by bit, they started packing up some of their Christmas decorations. The tree alone took two days to take down. The same crew who had put up the lights was scheduled to take them down in a few days.

The last two things to be put away were the snow globe and the crèche, both of which stayed up through the Day of Epiphany, January the sixth, the day which celebrates the wise men finding Jesus. It was a special day to Jillian in many ways, especially since it was her late mother's birthday.

Jillian had known about Epiphany before she ever heard anything about it in church or Sunday School. Her mom had always felt privileged having a birthday on that day, and had taught Jillian the story when she was a preschooler. Her mother was the only person she knew who had a "King's Cake" for her birthday cake. It always made the day extra special and fun, especially waiting to see who would find the small ceramic baby Jesus that had been baked into the cake.

Jillian used her grandmother's recipe, who had begun the tradition when her mom, Judy, was a little girl. She made the cake for John, and they had it, along with a cup of strong coffee, in honor of her mother. She hadn't had a baby Jesus to put in it, but used a dried bean instead, which was an alternative many bakers used. It was a nice observance, but had Jillian known the things that would happen in the next few days, she would have waited to celebrate.

First came a call from Pete. Gus and Grace were ready to come home! Jillian had never heard Pete as excited as he was on the phone that day. Initially, he had wanted her to come over, but Jillian convinced him that this was a very special moment that should be shared only with his wife and children. She would visit soon, in a day or two, but not that first afternoon and evening. That would be their special time, when they—Pete, Kelly, Gus, and Grace—learned how to be a family together for the very first time.

"You're right, Jillian. I never really thought of it that way. We're a family," he said in a tone of wonder.

"Yes, you are. Your life will never be the same again—in many ways. It will be hard. It will be wonderful. It will be everything in between," she said. "But you will experience all those things—together!"

"Together," he said, sounding completely amazed. "Jillian, I'm so happy. I don't know if I can take it."

"You can, Pete, and you will," she said. "You're a parent now. That's what parents do—they 'take it.'"

"Thanks, Jillian. I can, and I will," he said, sounding strong and ready for his new role in life, and all the surprises that go with it.

The next morning, Saturday, the phone rang in the library. Jillian was often tempted to have their landline discontinued, but at other times, it felt nice that there was at least one phone that wasn't attached to a purse or pocket at all times. She rushed to see who was calling.

The caller ID said it was Alan. Jillian wondered what was up. They had just been at his house earlier in the week, so maybe a new script had come to his attention, or there was an audition he wanted John to do. Alan was one happy man as of late. After two years of John not performing—not even auditioning—John was on an impressive roll, and that made Alan's world a much happier one.

Jillian answered the phone happily, "Good morning, Alan!"

"You've got that right, Jillian. It is a *very* good morning. Is your husband there?" he asked, excitement in his voice.

Jillian still smiled every time someone referred to John as her *husband*. Even after nine months, she had difficulty believing that she was really married, and it was even more difficult to believe that she was married to John—John D. Romano, who turned out to be one of the most talented, intelligent, caring, observant, and thoughtful people she had ever met. And best of all, the person who wanted to spend his life with her.

"Actually, Alan, he and Lucy are at the pet store. May I take a message, or have him call you when he gets home?" she asked. Lucy, the cat, and John were on what Jillian affectionately referred to as their "date morning," which now was only once a month rather than once a week as it had been when she first met John. Lucy had been his closest, and his *only,* companion for the two years that John disconnected himself from work, family, and friends. Weekly trips to the pet store with Lucy had been John's only activity outside of the house during those years. Now John struggled to find one morning a month to take Lucy to buy food, a special toy or treat, or sometimes for some special grooming.

"Well, I guess I could tell you..." Alan began.

"Wait a moment, Alan," Jillian interrupted. "If you have something important to tell John, I think you should tell him directly. He probably has his ringer off, but I will try to text him and tell him to call you."

"You are right, Jillian. I'll wait for his call. And Jillian, thanks for marrying John," Alan said.

"Oh, you'll never have to thank me for doing that, Alan. That was the best thing that ever happened to me," she said sincerely.

"And it was one of the best things that ever happened to me, too," he said, equally sincere.

"I'm glad to hear that," she said, chuckling. Seriously, she knew that two years of John not answering his phone calls from Alan would have been the end of most actor's associations with their agent, but Alan had never given up on John. He was more than an agent, he was a true friend. Jillian appreciated and liked the man, and his sweet wife, Beverly, very much. "I'll text him right away," she said.

"Thanks, Jillian. Have a great day," he said.

"You, too," she responded.

"Already done," he answered.

The phone call was killing Jillian. Alan sounded so excited. Whatever news he had, it was very good. She took out her cell, and her fingers flew over the keyboard as she informed John that he should call Alan as soon as possible.

Jillian didn't have to wait long. Only minutes after she texted John, he walked into the kitchen, Lucy in his arms.

"Did you two have a nice time together?" Jillian asked, feigning jealousy.

At the sound of Jillian's voice, the pretty orange feline bolted from John's arms and ran to her feet, where she purred and rubbed against Jillian's ankles. The cat had adored Jillian from their very first meeting.

"Lucy, you two-timer," John said, pretending to sound upset with the cat and walking toward the two "girls" in his life. "And after all I spent on you this morning!"

"She can't help it if she loves me, John," Jillian responded as John stopped in front of her.

John put his arms around Jillian. "Well, I certainly understand that. I can't help it either," he said, and kissed her softly. His words reminded her of a conversation she had with Marty after meeting John and Lucy for the first time. She had told Marty that for some reason, the cat seemed to like her. Marty's response had been that she didn't think the cat was the only one who liked her.

Jillian found it hard to pull back from John's embrace, but she wanted to know if he had called Alan, so she backed away gently, looking into his eyes as if they would give her an answer.

"Did you get my text message?" she asked.

"Not yet. I was driving. What does it say?" he said, kissing her between words.

"Hmmm," she said in response to his lips. "Alan wants you to call him A.S.A.P. It sounded important."

"More important than kissing my wife?" he asked, kissing her again.

Kathy J. Jacobson

"Now who's the two-timer? But seriously, as much as I am enjoying this, John, he really wanted to talk to you right away."

"Okay, okay, but I should get the cat food and other things in from the car first."

"I'll take care of that," Jillian said. "You call Alan."

"It really sounded that important?" John asked, his eyebrows arched.

She nodded. "Otherwise, I wouldn't be letting you go right now," she said, meaning it, and caressing his cheek.

He kissed her cheek quickly and reluctantly headed toward the library, most likely out of habit from years of using the landline phone in the room. Now, even when he used his cell, John liked to sit on the love seat, which had replaced his former favorite chair shortly after their marriage, to make phone calls.

"I want a raincheck," he called over his shoulder.

"Definitely," Jillian responded as she headed to the garage.

She carried in a case of Lucy's special diet food, bags of litter and boxes of healthy treats, and of course, a new toy. Jillian put them in their designated spots in the laundry room, then fed the cat, who was pacing around her personalized ceramic bowl in anticipation.

She pet Lucy, who was busy gobbling up her food. Then Jillian washed and dried her hands and headed toward the library.

John was not in the love seat when she arrived. Instead, he was standing next to the custom-built case which housed his Golden Globe and Emmy Awards. Jillian's heart started to pound as she sensed that something special was unfolding.

She heard John's final words before he ended the call.

"Not nearly as much as I do," he said, in an unusual tone.

Just then, John turned around and looked at Jillian. His eyes looked watery as she approached him.

"What did Alan say?" she asked softly, trying not to sound as excited as she felt inside.

"He said that he loves my wife... I told him not nearly as much as I do."

"What prompted that remark?" she asked, sliding her arms around John's waist.

"Oh, just a little news he received today. It appears..." He had to stop mid-sentence. "It appears," he said clearing his throat, "that I have been nominated for the Academy Award for Best Supporting Actor for my role as Mack." He looked, and sounded, stunned, and Jillian was on her way to that state as well.

Jillian had been quite certain that Alan had good news for John, but she hadn't imagined anything quite *that* good. It wasn't until she saw John standing next to the award case that the thought had flashed through her mind. An Academy Award—the one thing he had been unable to obtain thus far in his career, the one thing that John had always dreamed about—was now a possibility. The nomination, in itself, was a huge honor.

Tears of joy were forming in Jillian's eyes. She was so very happy for John. They both seemed at a loss for words, so they just held each other tightly.

Finally, they separated and looked into each other's faces. Jillian smiled at John. "I am *so* very proud of you, John," she said.

"I can't believe this is happening. First, I get back into acting and get the lead role in a play. Then I audition for a small part and end up as Mack. Now I'm doing a film with Carson Stone. And now this... it's all because of you..."

She cut him off right there. "John, this is *not* about me. You are the one who has earned this honor. You are the one who made Mack come alive, and all the other roles you play so instinctively and perfectly. You have such a gift, and I'm just so happy you are back and sharing it with the rest of the world. Now, if you want to nominate me for *best supporting spouse*, I'll gladly accept. But the rest—it's all *you*, John."

He held her close and so tightly she could barely breathe. He let go and looked at her. "I feel like my career—and my life—have completely started over."

She tilted her chin up toward his. "New creation," she said in almost a whisper.

He nodded, took her face in his hands, and gave her a kiss she would not soon forget.

Now it was Jillian's turn to wish she didn't have to go to work, but two bookstores were awaiting her presence. John lay next to her, sound asleep. She quietly slipped out from the sheets and took a quick shower, dressed and wrote John a note. Every once in a while she liked to do that, for old time's sake.

She put it where she was pretty certain he would see it, brushed her lips against his forehead, and was down the stairs and out the door to the garage. She opened the garage door and began backing up. She was turning the steering wheel when she hit the brakes, shocked to see people in her driveway. People with cameras. Paparazzi. Some took photos of her. Others shouted to her. "Where's John?" "What do you think of his Oscar nomination?" "Why are you leaving? Are you upset with him?"

She wasn't sure what to do. She rolled down the window of her vehicle and told the people to please move, as she needed to go to work. She also told them to please leave her property immediately, or she would call the authorities.

She started to slowly drive the Land Rover forward, the garage door closing behind her. They reluctantly started to move after she got her cell phone out and pretended to call the police.

This is only the beginning, isn't it? That was her thought as she turned onto the street and drove to the bookstore. On the way, she dialed one of the companies that had given them a quote for a new security system and for gating the front of the property. "How soon could you begin if we want to proceed?" she asked, sad at the thought but recognizing reality when she saw it.

The next day was crazy. There had been people in the driveway again at 4:15 a.m. when John left for the studio. John asked them to please leave, and told them he would be doing a press interview at six o'clock at his agent's office if they were interested. He also told them to please stay off his private property in the future. He called Jillian during a break that morning, and they decided to tell the security company to get to work as soon as possible. John also hired a security guard beginning immediately to keep people out of the driveway and front yard, at least until the nomination news frenzy died down.

John especially didn't want people around while he was in Alaska and Jillian was home alone. Suddenly he was wishing that Marty and Michael were still home, although they would have had to leave soon one way or the other as the semester was almost ready to begin. Carol, unfortunately, had to return to Madison as well to begin her final semester at the university. He thought about calling Pete and asking him to come over once in awhile, but he was both a new dad and business owner. John would just have to trust the hired guard to do the job.

Before John's departure to Alaska, he was invited to attend the Academy's "nominees luncheon." Luckily, Carson Stone, the director of John's current film, and another person working on the technical side of the movie were also attending. Carson had one of the assistant directors shoot some minor scenes and clean up some others in their absence. There was only one more day of shooting in Los Angeles after the lunch, then they were all on their way north.

John was absolutely beat when he came home at 8:30 p.m. the night before his departure. The newly-hired security guard met him at the base of the driveway. John parked the car in the garage and wearily walked into the kitchen where Jillian was waiting for him with a light dinner.

"You're a lifesaver," he said, noticing the food she had prepared. He gave her a kiss, then sat down at the breakfast nook.

"So are you," she said, sitting down across from him.

"You didn't have to wait for me. I know you don't like to eat this late," he said.

"That's why it's lighter fare," she replied, "although I doubt anything will keep you from sleeping after the schedule you've been keeping."

"You're probably right about that," he said, letting out a sigh. "There's been a lot of very early mornings. At least I won't be bothering you by getting up in the middle of the night after tomorrow morning."

"You never bother me, John."

He smiled and took her hand. "I love you, Mrs. Romano," he said.

"I love you, too, Mr. Romano," she replied.

"I wish I didn't have to leave you for two weeks." He sighed again, more heavily, "And I suppose I actually have to pack, too."

"All your clothes are clean, and your luggage is airing out in our room. I didn't know how much you were taking, but you can take your pick."

"Thanks, Jillian. You are so thoughtful," he said.

"Speaking of thoughts—I had one today. Why don't I go with you to Alaska? I can tell my agent I'm going there for family reasons," she suggested.

"Jillian, you don't need to cancel work on my account. Things are going so well for your book, and I don't want your agent to get upset with *you* because of *me*," he said sincerely.

"I don't think she'd be too upset," Jillian said. Jillian had been thinking about this Alaska trip a lot. She was not looking forward to John being so far away for two full weeks. To make things worse, she would be gone the following month for a couple of weeks. But if she was honest with herself, the biggest drawback was Monica. Jillian didn't relish the thought of how Monica might act once she was in Alaska. "Besides, maybe my presence up there would be helpful in keeping things in check," Jillian continued.

"By 'things,' are you talking about Monica?" John asked.

"Yes, I am. I just know how some people can be when they go away from home. I've been at too many medical conferences, I guess." Jillian was thinking of one in particular she had attended. One of her fellow nurses was interested in a married doctor. The nurse had been pursuing him to some extent at the hospital, but other people's discouragement helped keep her behavior at a reasonable level. But when they all went to Chicago for a weekend, the woman was, for lack of a better word, *crazed*.

She wouldn't leave the doctor alone. Finally, she convinced him to have a drink with her—just "as a friend." She proceeded to kiss him in front of a group of people at the hotel bar. It took little time before the word of the kiss got around. The doctor was divorced within the year. Jillian kept thinking of that determined look on Monica's face when she had come out of John's trailer at the studio. Unless she had truly changed over their holiday break, Jillian thought Monica had the potential to become *crazed* once they got far away from home.

"Jillian, I don't think you have anything to worry about. You know how much I love you," he said.

"I do. I don't worry about you, John. I trust you, but I can't say that I trust her, not completely at least. It could be a miserable couple of weeks if she starts back in..."

"She won't," John said confidently.

Jillian realized that this conversation was going nowhere, so she conceded.

"I hope you're right," she said, not sounding very convinced. And later she prayed that John would indeed be correct in his assumption.

Chapter Thirteen

The day John left for Alaska, Jillian "drowned her sorrows" in the sweet smell of newborns. She and Kelly took turns holding and feeding Gus and Grace, seated in two large, comfy rocking chairs at Pete and Kelly's home. Pete was at the gym, which was going so well that he had recently quipped that he was going to have "twins" again. He was presently looking for property for the building of a second "For Pete's Sake." Once it opened, Kelly planned to leave her current position and do marketing and other business work for the gyms, primarily from home. It was a "win-win" situation for everyone in the new family.

The babies were a great distraction. But once Jillian left Pete and Kelly's, she just couldn't seem to shake the nagging feeling that Monica was not going to be appropriate during this final on-location stretch, and when Jillian got strong feelings like that, they often came to fruition. She knew the past ten days had gone well, but John had also admitted that he had done minimal work with Monica during that time.

Speaking of work, Jillian had a lot of it to do while John was gone, which was helpful in some respects but stressful in others.

She was gathering more and more stories about people and their pregnancy/newborn losses. The newest additions were stories surrounding the issue of infertility. Some of those stories were just as heartbreaking as the ones about people who miscarried or had other types of pregnancy losses. Jillian knew that her own parents had gone through almost ten years of every kind of test and therapy known at that time, to no avail. In the end, it worked out all right, and she often thanked God that they couldn't conceive, or her life could have ended up much differently. They, too, were thankful for Jillian, and later Marty. They all felt that they were made for one another, although in the early years before they adopted, Martin and Judy Johnson had faced many disheartening moments.

Of course, there were many scheduled bookstore appearances, and lately more health organizations and churches wanted to know more about the book. Jillian had prepared different presentations for each venue. She was also slated to do a brief talk and signing at "For Pete's Sake." Pete was really getting into a holistic approach to good health at his gym, which Jillian thought might be why it was doing so well. The people who went there seemed to feel encouraged toward healthy living on many different levels and aspects of their lives, and seemed appreciative of Pete's efforts and concern for their total well-being.

When Jillian got home later that afternoon, she felt absolutely lost. She hadn't felt like that in a really long time. She could barely remember her life before John anymore. Their lives were both independent, yet integrally intertwined. They loved each other, supported each other, and brought out the best in one another. Jillian used to inwardly scoff at people who spoke about finding their "soul mate," but now she understood that it was a real thing, and she greatly missed hers.

As if he were reading her mind, her cell phone rang. John's name flashed across its face.

"Hi, sweetheart," Jillian said. "I was just thinking about you."

"I could tell," he said sweetly. "We made it to our lodge—finally," he said. "It's very rustic-looking, but quite nice inside. But boy, is it *cold* outside!"

"You've been away from the Midwest too long, John. You're soft," she said teasingly.

"I know. And it will be even colder sleeping without you tonight," he said.

Jillian was not looking forward to sleeping alone either, and was certain that even in the warmer climate of California, it would be a very cold night without John at her side. Jillian wanted to remind him that she offered to come, but she decided not to reopen that can of worms. Instead, she softly replied, "I agree."

John told her about the plane ride to Anchorage, then taking a smaller plane to Valdez, which had been a bit on the bumpy side. The cast and crew had been bussed up to the lodge, had checked in, and would soon have dinner. Afterward, they had a meeting to make sure everyone was on the same page for early the next morning. It was dark there already, even though it was an hour earlier than Los Angeles. There was little daylight to work with, so scenes taking place in the lodge, the makeshift studio, and the interior of the pipeline facilities would be done when it was dark. The other ones would be shot during the short six hours of daylight.

If it hadn't been for the fact that they had a production schedule to meet and other obligations awaiting a number of people involved in the project, they might have picked a different month to shoot. However, from a lodging standpoint, the place where they were staying had more vacancies at this time of year, so it worked great for a production crew and was beneficial to the lodge. The wintry scenery also made a breathtaking backdrop for their story.

A crew had gone up a week early to create an indoor studio out of an old airplane hanger next to the lodge. In it they manufactured half of a cabin, open from the side, and several other rooms featured in the movie. It was all quite impressive, John informed Jillian.

"Sorry, I've got to go, Jillian. They are calling us to dinner. I'll love you forever," he said.

"I'll love you forever," she said back, feeling tearful as she hit the "end call" button.

One other positive diversion during John's absence was Jillian's meeting with Marianna, the young woman who worked in a dress shop. Marianna had helped Jillian pick out more than one perfect dress for a special occasion. They made an appointment at the store one morning, and Jillian tried on a few formal dresses, but none of the options seemed right—at least not for "Oscar Night," as they both referred to it.

"I could make you something," Marianna finally said.

"Really? It's only three weeks away," Jillian remarked.

"I've made things in a shorter time than that. I have a project for school I'm working on, but I could fit this in, if you would like."

"I would definitely *like!*" Jillian retorted.

The two met later that afternoon at the house. Marianna's eyes were huge when she stepped inside. They went into the library, where there was good natural light coming in from the many windows. Marianna's eyes got even bigger as she saw the glass showcase with the awards in it.

"Are you sure you want *me* to do this, Ms. Romano?"

"Jillian, remember? Definitely. You have impeccable taste and talent. Let's see what you brought," Jillian said, glancing at the book Marianna had under her arm.

"These are my favorite designs. I've marked the pages with the ones I thought would look best on you," Marianna said, starting to become more at ease. They began to look through them, making notes on another sheet of paper.

They came to one that both of them really liked. "If I got to choose just one of these for you, Ms. ... Jillian, this is the one," she said.

"Then that's the one I want," Jillian said. They talked about color options and chose one. Then Marianna got out her measuring tape and carefully took Jillian's measurements. She wanted this to be just right. She said she was going to the fabric store the next day and would begin working on it right away, so they could have a fitting soon and make certain that it was acceptable.

Jillian could tell the young woman was very serious about this project, and also very excited. It isn't every day someone gets to make a dress for "Oscar Night." Then again, Jillian thought, it's not every day someone's husband is up for an Academy Award. She still had trouble believing that it was really happening.

Jillian took Marianna home after the session, and was happy to see that the press was nowhere in sight. She wondered if they had followed John to Alaska. She wouldn't put it past them.

The next day there was no call from John, which considering their schedule, wasn't that surprising. But when she didn't get one the next day, she began to worry. She texted him, hoping that it would be delivered. She wasn't sure how well mobile phones worked up there, especially outside of the lodge. She got no response, and thought perhaps he had no service.

Finally, the next day, the long-awaited call from John rang on her cell.

"Jillian, I'm so sorry I haven't talked to you in two days. I got your text when I got back to the lodge last night, but it was so late I didn't want to call. Are you okay?"

"That's what I was going to ask you?" she said.

He hesitated, and she knew that something was up.

"Oh, just the usual very long days of filming. It's beautiful during the day, even the snow, but still pretty cold." His voice sounded like he was trying to avoid something.

"How is everything else?"

"Oh, the scenes are going pretty well. There are quite a few action scenes, and I even have a stunt double for one. That's a first."

Jillian wished he could have a "stunt double" for his other "action" scenes, like the kisses and the one she was dreading the most, the bedroom scene he and Monica would be shooting any day now. It was obvious to Jillian that if Monica was behaving poorly, John was not ready to share that information quite yet, so she told him about Marianna and the dress instead.

"That's sounds great, Jillian. She certainly has good taste in that area, if I remember correctly," he said.

Jillian smiled at that. "I miss you, John," she said.

"I miss you, too. I'm marking off the days on a little calendar they had in my 'welcome basket' on the bed in my room when I arrived. Only twelve more days of shooting, then I get to come home."

They said their usual "good night" to one another and hung up. Twelve days sounded like an awfully long time to Jillian. Little did she know that it sounded like an absolute eternity—and not a heavenly one—to her husband.

Monica Morgan was in rare form in Alaska. If John had thought she was bad during the early weeks of taping in L.A., it was ten times worse on location. Just as Jillian had predicted, Monica would aggressively seek him at every opportunity.

It had all begun with innuendo the very first day on the set. Then it was things like Monica being in the hallway near his room wearing only her robe. Thank goodness no one else seemed to be around when that happened—the paparazzi would feast on something like that. In the buffet line, she would "accidentally" bump into him, or come up behind him quietly so when he turned around, he was face-to-face with her.

But the intimate scenes between them were the worst. During the last kissing scene, she had been very inappropriate. But the bedroom scene was the worst of all. John hadn't quite known how to approach that one. It was tough to be in this scene with someone with whom he had once had a relationship. It was even tougher to be in one with someone he currently was on the verge of *loathing*. And it was difficult not to think of Jillian and her fears about Monica. Had Monica come to Alaska acting like a decent human being and a professional actor, it wouldn't have been as bad, but she was at her very worst—exactly what his wife had feared.

They tried a couple of takes of the bedroom scene, with no success. Monica, of course, made a number of crude and cruel remarks. John thought that perhaps the only way he could get through this scene was to imagine that it was Jillian he was with, but that proved to be a poor solution and caused even more trouble. In the middle of the scene, Monica made the remark, "I knew you still liked me!" That was it for John. He sat up on the side of the bed and said he was done with the scene. Carson Stone was not happy with either one of them and informed them that they *were* going to get this right, sooner or later.

They broke for dinner and John went to call Jillian.

"Hi, honey," Jillian said in a perky voice. She had had a great time at "For Pete's Sake" that afternoon. There were more people who came to hear what she had to say than she ever would have imagined. She also sold some books, which was nice, but the best thing was just the way people listened and seemed to be seriously considering her stories and words of advice.

"Jillian," he said. "It's so good to hear your voice."

"It's so good to hear yours, too, but what's wrong?" She was getting almost as good at reading her husband's voice as she was her daughter's.

"It's Monica," he said. "I was wrong, you were right, and I sure wish you were here."

She could hear one of the crew members telling John that Carson wanted to talk to him before dinner, so John had to hang up.

John's words, "I sure wish you were here," were all it took for Jillian. As soon as they hung up, she called her agent and cancelled her schedule for the next week-and-a-half, using the excuse of an important family matter, which was the truth. Then she called the airline.

Chapter Fourteen

Jillian dug out her down vest, fleece jacket, hat, gloves, and scarf from the back of the closet. She hadn't worn them since she left Wisconsin and had almost given them away. At the last minute, she changed her mind, thinking she might need them for occasional trips back to the Midwest to see family and friends, or ventures to the mountains. She never dreamed she would be using them to go to Alaska in the middle of winter.

The first leg of the trip to Anchorage was uneventful. The second part, the flight to Valdez, was exactly the opposite. Jillian texted John when she arrived in Anchorage, just so he would have some idea that she was on her way to him and what time she was expected to arrive in Valdez. She knew he had filming late and told him that she had transportation set up with the lodge, so he need not worry. Little did she know, he would end up being almost out of his mind with worry by the end of the evening.

Jillian was on the final flight of the three that flew into Valdez each day. As they buckled their seat belts, the Captain casually mentioned that they should be getting to their destination "just ahead of the big storm." Jillian was not a huge fan of flying in winter in general, but the thought of flying just ahead of a winter storm made her heart leap.

The first fifteen minutes of the flight were bumpy, but she expected that after her earlier conversation with John. The next forty-five minutes were some of the most terrifying of her life.

The pilot had come on the intercom and told everyone that the storm was coming in faster than expected, and to "hold on tight." Jillian's heart was pounding, and her stomach was roiling. She closed her eyes, clenched the armrests of the plane with cold, sweaty palms, and prayed without ceasing for the remainder of the trip. She didn't stop until they came to a stop, which felt like a lifetime later. It was the worst landing she could ever remember experiencing, with a lot of loud thumps, and slipping and sliding all over the runway. But finally, the plane came to a complete halt.

Every person on board looked like a zombie as they deplaned. She was certain that she was as white as the down vest she was wearing. She waited for her backpack to be carried in, then looked for the driver from the lodge. She found him talking to a woman working the desk at the tiny airport. He was none too happy to be out on a night like this. He grumbled as they climbed into a huge four-wheel drive vehicle with gigantic chains on the tires, and took off slowly to the resort. Jillian felt bad that she had made him drive in weather like this, but she had not known the forecast. She apologized, then sat quietly the rest of the trip, trying not to worry about ending up in a ditch on top of everything else.

The snow was nearly a whiteout by the time they made it to the lodge. The man carried in her bag without saying a word. Jillian gave him a good tip for his trouble, then introduced herself to the woman at the front desk and asked where the production crew was currently working. Luckily, it was at the old hanger-turned-studio, which was right next to the lodge.

She decided that she would go straight to it and let John know that she had arrived. He may not even know what was going on outside, she thought. In fact, she hoped that he didn't.

But he did know. John had been in a major panic for the past hour-and-a-half. People kept coming in with the latest weather reports, and he was going out of his mind. Monica was still up to her antics, and they were struggling with a kissing scene. In the scene, Monica's character came to the door of his character's cabin. His character had been worried about her character, and he was supposed to be very glad to see her, then kiss her.

Jillian walked up to an assistant watching the scene and put down her backpack. She heard the director say the scene number and take—seven—which is never a good sign.

"Are you Jillian?" the woman asked.

"I am," she said.

"Thank God! I thought he was going to kill her," she said seriously.

"That bad, huh?"

"Yes, but maybe now that you're here..." she said, waving her arms at John.

John finally noticed the woman, then he saw Jillian. The look of frantic worry turning instantly to relief was not one Jillian would soon forget.

The director yelled, "Let's roll," and John turned back to his scene.

Monica knocked on the fake cabin door, and John opened it. She stepped in, he looked relieved to see her, took her in his arms, and planted a huge kiss on her lips.

The director shouted, "Cut! That's a wrap! Take five!"

Monica started to say, "Now, that's more like it..." to John, but he practically dropped her and ran toward Jillian, hurdling over a couple of props as he bounded across the studio.

Jillian and the production assistant were standing behind a line, where those not in the scene were supposed to stay. John stopped at the line and held out his hands to Jillian, who grabbed onto them like she was holding on for dear life.

"Thank God you are all right," he said, squeezing her hands. Jillian didn't feel all right, but she didn't say that. "I'd come over there, but Carson would kill me if I had to go back to makeup," John added, rubbing his thumbs over the tops of her hands, his eyes penetrating hers.

Jillian had never been so happy to see anyone in her life. "It sounds like it's been a tough night of shooting," she remarked.

John nodded in acknowledgement. "It won't be, now that I know you are here and safe."

The director called the actors back to their places.

"We have to do the bedroom scene again, Jillian. It hasn't been going very well. You don't have to watch this if you don't want to. I can give you a key to the room."

"No, I want to watch, John," she said. It wasn't completely the truth, but she knew she was already in a traumatized state, so what did it really matter? "If it's all right with you," she tacked on.

"If you are okay with it, I'm okay with it," he said. She knew that look on his face. He wanted to kiss her, and she wanted to kiss him, but they couldn't. Even if they could cross the line, it wouldn't be professional behavior, so it would have to wait.

She forced a little smile. "Go on."

He squeezed her hands one more time, then turned to go to the "bedroom" section of the fake cabin and began to unbutton his shirt. Suddenly Jillian wasn't so sure she really did want to see this, but it was too late now.

The production assistant came back and stood next to her again after John moved back to the set. "What does it feel like to have someone love you that much?" she asked sincerely.

Jillian only needed one word to respond, "Heavenly."

The assistant, whose name was Jamie, quietly brought over John's chair for Jillian to sit in and positioned it so that she could see the scene, and those in it could see her, including Monica.

The first thing Monica asked as she and John got ready to climb into the bed was, *"Who is that?"*

"That—she—is Jillian, my beautiful wife."

Monica's only response was, "Oh."

Jillian was not looking forward to watching John kiss the still striking woman with the model's body, but once they got the cameras rolling, she wondered how anyone could perform in a scene like that with all the bright lights, people staring at them, and knowing it was being filmed. It took real talent, and she tried to concentrate on that aspect. The lights and cameras also helped her to remember that it was not real, but pretend. And the thought that she was the one who got to experience "reality" made her feel better.

The hardest part of the situation was knowing that once upon a time, there *was* a "reality" between John and Monica, too. But then she remembered that she, herself, had a child, and that was a "reality" also, and that the father of that child was not a factor in her life now, just as Monica was not one in John's life anymore outside of work. Jillian focused on all these things, and before she knew it, the director was shouting in a very relieved tone, "That's a wrap! Have a good night, everybody!"

John came over to her, helped her out of her chair, picked up the backpack, and took her hand. They walked quietly back to the lodge. It was a good thing it was only about fifty yards away, as they could barely see where they were going. They hustled—as quickly as one can go in snow that kept on filling the sidewalk as fast as the maintenance crew tried to clear it—inside the building.

Inside, a roaring fire was going in the biggest fireplace Jillian had ever laid eyes on. It was like night and day between the outside world and the inside world.

They didn't speak as they headed up a huge open staircase to the second floor. John unlocked the door, and they stepped inside a large room that was warm and felt homey. He put the backpack down on the floor, and pulled Jillian into his arms and held her tightly. He stroked her hair with his hand. It was wet because of the snow and a mess because of the wind, but John didn't care. Then he gently kissed her forehead.

"I was so worried about you," he said, in almost a whisper. Jillian didn't say anything, because she had been pretty worried herself, and she knew he would sense it in her voice if she spoke. "If anything ever happened to you, I think I would die," he added, sounding upset.

"John, you wouldn't die," she said softly. "You'd be sad—really sad—but promise me that if anything ever does happen, you will go on with all the things we have always planned to do."

"I promise," he said looking into her eyes, his face still full of concern, "but I hope I never have to face that situation."

"So do I."

"I love you so much, Jillian," he said, and pulled her close to kiss her.

"I love you, too, John," she replied, just before their lips met.

The almost-a-week apart from each other had felt endless to Jillian. She missed his kisses. She missed the warmth of his body next to hers every night. She missed his gentle touch.

He pulled back reluctantly. "Do you mind if I run through the shower real quick? I need to shower off..." He stopped, not knowing how to proceed with his words, but Jillian understood and nodded her head for him to go. She wanted him to shower off "Monica" just as much as he did.

He rushed into the bathroom, emerging just a few minutes later in a robe from the lodge.

"My turn," she said, just as he was about to grab her. She didn't want to say that she needed to wash off the smell of deathly fear, but that was exactly what she needed to do. She still didn't feel very well, but certainly better than she had two hours before.

Jillian was equally quick in the shower. She brushed her teeth, noticing that John must have done the same. He had even used mouthwash, not his usual practice, but when she considered the scene he had just completed, she considered it a thoughtful thing to do.

When Jillian came out of the bathroom, John was standing in front of a large mirror and staring into it with a grave look on his face.

"That's a pretty serious look on your face, Mr. Romano," she said, coming up behind him and putting her arms around him.

"I was just wondering what kind of man makes his wife have to fly up to Alaska in a horrendous snowstorm, just because he was too pigheaded to listen to her in the first place and accept her gracious offer to join him. This is all my fault," he said.

"John, it's not your fault that there was a snowstorm, and that it came in faster than even the weather service thought it would."

He turned around to her. "Jillian, would you forgive me for having—what was it that Edith called it—a 'stupid spell?'"

Jillian knew what her almost ninety-five-year-old friend would tell her to do, and she pulled him close. "I think that could be arranged," she said, slightly playing with him and beginning to feel more like herself again.

He looked at her so seriously. "This must have been a pretty awful night for you. First, you have a horrible flight, then you arrive just in time to see me hop into bed with another woman. Did it bother you too much to watch that last scene?" he asked.

"Not as much as I thought it would. I decided that I'd better get used to it, because it's probably just the beginning of many. Once this movie comes out, my prediction is that you are going to be in many more movies, and probably many more scenes just like it. I also decided that at the end of the day, as long as you come home to *me*, and that I'm the *only* one who gets to do *this*," she said, and kissed him, "that I will be okay. Deal?"

"Deal," he said softly, then kissed her with a passion that made the snowstorm outside look tame.

Chapter Fifteen

J illian didn't even hear John get up, but was awakened when he gently kissed her goodbye.

"I'm sorry, I didn't mean to wake you up," he said. "I've got to go to makeup. There's breakfast from six until nine in the dining room. Just give them our room number. I should be back in time for lunch, so I'll meet you in the lobby around 12:30."

He caressed her face. "I don't want to go," he told her, and then kissed her.

Jillian pulled him down and held him for a moment. She didn't want him to go either, and kissed his cheek. "You'd better go," she said reluctantly.

"Yes, I'd better, because if I don't..." He finished his sentence by kissing her. He groaned as he forced himself to stand up and leave. He turned back to her as he reached the door.

"I'm so glad you're here, Mrs. Romano."

"So am I."

John practically jumped into the chair in the makeup room.

"Good morning, Samantha!" he exclaimed to the makeup artist, a big smile stretched across his face.

"My, aren't we chipper this a.m." Samantha replied. For the past few days, she had seen him become more and more disgruntled, especially if he had to be anywhere near Monica Morgan.

Just then, Monica came into the room. She took a chair several seats away from John this time, and didn't even look his way. Another makeup artist, also a "Sam," but a male one, started brushing out her long, luminous blonde hair. John glanced at her, thinking that she looked very tired and unhappy.

"Good morning," he said to her, to be polite.

"Good morning," she replied quietly, but that was all. No smart retort, no inappropriate remark, just a simple good morning. It was a refreshing change for John and for the others in the room, who were expecting the usual rude or off-color remark.

John and Samantha talked quite a bit that morning, mostly about her family. He had never really asked much about them before, and Samantha seemed very pleased as she relayed the latest exploits of her twelve-year-old son and ten-year-old daughter.

When the two actors were done in their chairs and walked away, Samantha asked Sam, "What happened to him?"

"I don't think it's a 'what,' I think it's a 'who.' I heard his wife came to spend some time with him," Sam said.

"I hope his wife sticks around." Samantha said as she put away her equipment.

Jillian slept until 7:30 a.m., got ready for the day, and headed down to the lodge dining hall. It wasn't too busy, as a portion of the cast and crew was out shooting a scene. There were some who were not "called" yet, however. One was the production assistant, Jamie, who had been so kind to Jillian upon her arrival.

As Jamie and Jillian walked toward the buffet, she asked Jamie if she could join her.

"Of course, Ms. Romano," she said.

"Please, call me Jillian," Jillian told her.

They had just joined the line for the buffet when the actor, Chase Cheekwood, came striding into the room, causing heads to turn, particularly among the females. Chase Cheekwood was handsome and talented—and he knew it. He had quite a reputation, not only for his work on the screen but with women. Jillian remembered one writer referring to him as "Chase *Cheatwood*." He had been married again this past year, for the third time in his forty years of life, a series of affairs having ended his first two marriages.

He *was* good-looking, there was no doubt about that. He had thick, ash blonde hair that many women would kill for. It had a natural wave, and it framed his chiseled face and bright, gray-green eyes. His complexion was ruddy, and his shoulders looked like they belonged to a linebacker. There was an air of confidence and swagger about him that definitely caught one's attention and made him seem larger than life in some ways.

He walked near Jamie and Jillian, then noticing Jillian, he stopped.

"You're new, aren't you?" he asked. He reminded her of the star basketball player at her high school, who was the boy everyone— except Jillian—had wanted to date.

"I haven't been 'new' for a long time," Jillian found herself retorting.

He chuckled, "Oh, good one. Chase Cheekwood," he said, extending his hand to her.

She shook it. "Jillian Johnson—*Romano*," she said, pausing and putting emphasis on that part of her last name.

"Right." "I'll be seeing you around, Jillian Johnson *Romano*," he said, smiling at her and adding a little wink.

Chase moved on past them. Jillian looked at Jamie, who appeared to be completely star-struck.

"He talked to you, Jillian! Isn't he just the most attractive man you've ever seen?" she asked.

"There is no doubt he is *physically* attractive," Jillian said, "but I can't say that I find a married man, who is flirting with a married woman, *attractive*."

"Oh, I never thought about it that way," Jamie replied.

Jillian thought that a lot of people didn't seem to think about things that way in the Hollywood scene.

"Maybe if more people thought about it that way, there wouldn't be so many painful relationships in this world," Jillian said calmly. Jamie seemed to consider those words, and gently nodded her head in agreement as they reached the enormous and elaborate breakfast bar.

Jillian was happy to see that they actually had something healthy on it along with the eggs, breakfast meats, made-to-order omelets, and flapjacks. She helped herself to some oatmeal with fresh fruit and nuts, and some fresh grilled fish. She and Jamie sat down, where Jillian found out that Jamie had come to California hoping to write screenplays, but had had no success at breaking in thus far. At least she was working in "the business," as she put it.

After breakfast, Jamie had to go to work. Jillian went back to her room, got her winter wear, and practically ran down the steps to the front desk. The storm had passed, and she needed some fresh air. She had noticed a sign that said there were snowshoes available, so she checked out a pair and went outside for her first true winter walk in over a year.

She had to admit that the pristine, new fallen snow, with the sun sparkling like diamonds on it, was breathtaking, and the brisk air was exhilarating. The scenery reminded her somewhat of

Wisconsin, and for a slight moment, she felt homesick. In her mind, she saw her dad pulling her on a sled when she was a young child, then as she got older, tobogganing down the big hill in her hometown, screaming and laughing intermittently all the way down.

Then there was her favorite winter activity of all, ice skating. Both of her parents liked doing that, even after her mom slipped one time getting onto the ice, breaking her arm. She wondered if there was skating at the lodge or anywhere nearby. She decided that would be one of the first things she inquired about when she got back.

After an hour-and-a-half outside, she was ready to get back to the warmth of the lodge. She retrieved her computer from her room and headed to a chair in front of the huge fireplace. She got herself situated, then began typing away, filling in her blog readers about her harrowing experience on the airplane the previous day. It seemed to Jillian like it happened a million years ago, thanks mostly to a night spent in John's loving and reassuring arms.

Again, as she did almost every day of her marriage, she wondered how she could possibly love someone so much, and be so loved. After so many years of fighting falling in love, of not letting her heart be open to that kind of risk, she was so incredibly thankful that God had somehow helped her take that leap of faith, and that this time her leap was with the "right person." Even in the past two months with this "Monica business," she never had a doubt that she had made the right decision to love again, and especially to love John.

Just thinking about him made her look at her watch. It was noon. Soon he would be back and meet her for lunch. She closed her laptop and bounded up the staircase to their room to freshen up. It had only been seven hours, but she missed him dearly.

At 12:30 p.m., a crowd of loudly talking people clamored through the doors of the lodge. She could tell by their smiles and banter that things must have gone well this morning, and she was glad for John and for the entire crew.

John walked over to her. His eyes twinkled in the bright lights of the lodge ceiling and the fire. She could tell he wanted to hug and kiss her, but she also knew that he was at work.

"Shall we?" he asked, and put out his arm to escort her to the dining room. She was surprised he was even willing to show that amount of affection in public. Just as they were walking in, Carson Stone asked if he could talk to John.

John nodded to Carson and turned disappointedly to Jillian. "I'm sorry. The director is beckoning."

"I'll wait inside the dining room and see you in a bit," she said.

"If I'm not there soon, begin without me. I'll catch up," he replied with that charming grin of his.

Jillian waited inside the door for ten minutes, then grabbed a tray and went through the line. She chose a grilled "freshly caught salmon" salad. She couldn't imagine that it could get any better than having the local fare, and she wouldn't be disappointed.

She looked around at the tables. There were no completely open tables, but there were a number of them with two or more open spots. And then there was one table with a lone diner sitting at it. Monica.

Jillian hesitated a moment, but something inside her guided her in Monica's direction. Monica looked, as Jillian's mother would have put it, "like a lost soul."

She said a little prayer as she slowly walked across the room toward Monica's table. "May I join you?" Jillian asked.

Monica jumped, startled by the question, and even more so by the person who was asking it. She reluctantly nodded her head affirmatively and seemed to squirm in her seat as Jillian sat down across from her. Jillian thought that if Monica could have, she would have run away—far away.

They sat silently for a moment. Jillian was aware of a number of people watching them at the table. Perhaps they were hoping that a good fight would break out, like one of those on some so-called "reality" shows.

Jillian was the one who broke the ice. "Was it a good shoot this morning?" she asked, knowing that Monica and John had been in an outdoor scene together.

"Yes, all went well," she said quietly. Monica sat staring at her plate, pushing her food around like a little girl who didn't want to eat her peas.

"I'm glad to hear it," Jillian said sincerely. Monica did not respond to this. Instead, she took a sip of water, then returned to maneuvering the morsels on her plate. They ate in silence another minute. Jillian decided that she would let Monica make the next move, if there was going to be one, in the conversation.

Finally, Monica put her fork down and looked at Jillian. For such a gorgeous woman, she looked worn and haggard, and Jillian saw pain in her eyes. Perhaps it was all those years of nursing, or perhaps the mission field or shut-in visits, but whatever the reason, Jillian knew the look of hurt in someone's eyes. Or maybe, she thought, it was from looking in the mirror for many of those years, when her own heart had laid in pieces.

Finally, Monica spoke. "I'm sorry," she said very quietly but also very sincerely, looking Jillian in the eye.

"Apology accepted. I forgive you," Jillian said, which made Monica's head snap back in surprise. Jillian continued, "But I'm not the one that really needs to hear that, Monica." Of course, she was referring to John.

Monica did not respond to that, but her eyes misted over.

"Monica, I don't know what is going on in your life right now. I know what I hear or read, but I also know from my own experience how inaccurate that can be. I believe you are in a lot of pain right now, but making my life or John's life or anyone else's life miserable is only going to cause more pain--not only for them but also for *you*," Jillian said.

Monica seemed to be considering what Jillian had just said, just as John stood looking around the room for Jillian, a full tray in his hands. He stopped short when he saw his wife sitting at a table—with Monica. He couldn't believe it. Maybe it was the only place available when Jillian had come in, but he looked around and there appeared to be numerous other open spots. He hesitantly began to head their way.

As John moved in the direction of Monica and Jillian, more heads were turning and watching the scenario, hoping that maybe it was finally going to "get good," but they would soon be disappointed and go back to their lunches.

Just before John got to the table, Jillian said one more thing to Monica. "I'm praying that things get better for you and your family soon."

Then John was there, and with a look of disbelief on his face, he took a seat between Monica and Jillian at the table meant for four. He couldn't believe he was going to have lunch sitting between his wife and his ex-lover.

A moment after John sat down, Jillian looked at her watch.

"Oh, my goodness! I forgot! I have to call my agent. I'm sorry, please excuse me," she said, standing up. She put her hand on John's shoulder, giving it a little squeeze. He put his hand on hers, like he was trying to keep her there and not leave him alone with this woman who had caused him so much pain, both in the past and in the present.

"I'll be in the room," she said, and then in a flash, Jillian was gone.

John wasn't sure what had just happened. He couldn't be certain, but he was pretty sure his wife had purposely put him in this awkward position.

He took a sip of coffee, then began to eat his salmon salad slowly. He had been starving when he had gotten in line, but now he had little appetite. *What was Jillian thinking?*

Monica took a sip of her water again, then cleared her throat.

"John," she said, then paused. "I..." She had to pause again. Clearly whatever she had to say was not easy for her to get out.

"John, I would like to apologize. I have behaved badly, and not just these last two months. I behaved badly when we were together. I was not faithful to you, and I ended our relationship poorly. So, I'm sorry. I hope someday you can forgive me," she said.

A forkful of salmon stopped midway between John's plate and his mouth. He was pretty sure that his mouth was hanging wide open and made a conscious effort to shut it. He sat there a moment, processing, as he so often did when others spoke to him. He wished that he could hit a replay button to make sure, but he was pretty certain that Monica Morgan had just apologized to him. It was the first time he had ever heard the words "I'm sorry" come out of her mouth in the thirty-some years he had known her—to anyone—and she certainly had never said it to him.

He felt stunned, but in a good way. Now it was his turn to stammer. "Monica...I...I accept your apology." Then he tacked on quietly, "Thank you."

"No, John. Thank you," she replied. Then she got up, took her tray, and tried to smile. "See you on the set," she said, and walked out of the room. Others watched her go, but since there were no outbursts or ridiculous displays, they quickly moved on with their own business.

John sat a moment, then quickly finished his salad, gulped down his coffee, grabbed the apple off his tray for later, and flew up the stairs to his room, taking two steps at a time. He felt light as a feather, like a giant burden had been lifted from his shoulders, one that had been there for a really long time.

John unlocked the door to the room and stepped inside. Jillian stood with her back to him, and she was indeed on the telephone. At the sound of the door opening, Jillian turned around toward John and smiled at him.

"Goodbye, sweetheart. I love you, too," she said to her daughter on the phone, and ended her call.

John walked up to her, put his hands on her waist and his forehead against hers. "Your agent?" he asked.

"How did you know?" Jillian answered.

John kissed her forehead and pulled her tightly against his body, putting his cheek to hers. His "five o'clock shadow," part of his new style for the film, felt rough, but for whatever reason, Jillian liked it. He stroked her back, but was silent.

Finally, he pulled back and looked at her, astonishment in his eyes. "Monica—just apologized to me," he said. "And I forgave her," he added, with equal disbelief.

"I'm so glad, John."

"You are the most amazing person I've ever known, Mrs. Romano."

"Well, then we're even," she said, and kissed him.

He kissed her, then kissed her again. He looked at his watch and said, "Oh no! I've got to be downstairs in three minutes. Will you come along with us, Jillian? We're going out to one of the stations along the pipeline. It should be very interesting."

"Let me get my jacket," she said, and kissed him one more time, and added as she usually said to him when they were interrupted, "Hold that thought."

"You'd better believe it," he replied.

They climbed onto the production bus. Chase Cheekwood was one of the first people Jillian saw as she walked down the center aisle.

"Jillian!" Chase called out. "Glad you could join us!"

She nodded her head to him and noticed her husband do a double-take. John had no idea that Jillian and Chase had met that morning, as he had been gone when their meeting had occurred. He gave Jillian a questioning look as they slid into a seat.

Reading her husband's mind, she said, "We met at breakfast this morning."

"Oh," was John's only response.

The drive was an hour away from the lodge. It seemed even shorter than that as the views were outstanding. The natural beauty of the area was stunning, but there was always the unspoken fear looming. If something happened to the pipeline, it would cause a natural disaster like none ever known to that area and beyond.

It was a true dilemma. The pipeline employed many people and was hugely important to the economy. It produced a needed commodity. It also posed a threat to nature. There were no simple answers to the controversies surrounding this project and others like it. There were many different angles to consider and many risks to be evaluated, including the possibility of terrorism, which was part of the movie's plot. The film John was making did a good job of examining the various sides of the issue.

Kathy J. Jacobson

The crew set up the scene quickly. There was going to be a fight scene involving the characters that Chase Cheekwood and John were playing against two of the villains in the story. Chase and John were playing the "good guys." The scene took place outside the substation, where there were many vents and tanks.

Jillian enjoyed how realistic they made the fight look, without even touching each other. All of a sudden, in one moment, all of that changed. Chase turned the wrong way, his hand smacked a metal tank, and there was a sickening pop. He had dislocated his middle finger and was screaming in agony. Jillian had seen strong athletes brought to their knees by dislocations. The malady was worse in some ways than a broken bone. The pain could be excruciating, especially if one did not have a high threshold of pain, which was apparently the case with Chase. He was at the opposite end of the pain tolerance spectrum, based on his near-hysterical behavior.

The injured actor sat in the snow, rocking back and forth, shouting, swearing, and screaming, with tears streaming down his face. He yelled that he was going to get sick, which was indeed within the realm of possibilities.

"Oh, good Lord!" Carson Stone shouted in a disgusted tone. "What are we going to do now? It's an hour to anywhere, and who knows how far to a clinic beyond that. And the man is absolutely mad with pain."

Jillian was already approaching the scene when John looked at her with an expression that said "help."

"Do we have any blankets around here, or extra coats or something?" Jillian asked, afraid that if Chase kept going the way he was, he might actually go into shock. She had seen stranger things happen with people who didn't do well with pain.

Someone ran up with a woolen blanket, and she put it around Chase's shoulders. She knelt down in front of him and talked calmly to him.

"Chase, you are going to be all right," she said in a reassuring tone.

"All right!" he barked, and let out an expletive. "I can't do this for an hour-and-a-half. I'm going to be sick."

"Chase, under normal circumstances, I wouldn't even offer this, but these are not normal circumstances. If you want me to, I can pull it back into place, but I want your permission, and I need a few other people here to hear you give me that permission, okay?" Jillian said.

"Please, help me! Yes, you can do it. I give you my full permission. Now please, help me." He was still rocking and sobbing.

She looked to the others around, and they agreed that they heard him. She had John and one of the actors who was playing a villain help Chase stand up, and each man held him under one of his arms.

"Chase, it's going to get worse before it gets better. Are you still okay with that? It's going to hurt for a moment even more than it hurts right now, but it should start to get better after that."

"It can't be any worse than this," he sobbed.

"Yes, it can, but only briefly. Are you ready? I'm going to count to ten," Jillian said, and started counting. On the count of four, she yanked his finger back into place. He let out a bloodcurdling scream, then almost passed out. John and the other actor caught him. They sat him back down onto the ground and put the blanket back around him.

"Do you have any cold packs, or a bag we could fill with ice or snow, and a towel or cloth?" Jillian asked the crew. "And we should get him back onto the bus and turn on the heat. Either that or go inside the substation."

Someone tried the door, but the station was locked. So John the other actor, whose name was Jack but everyone called him "Jones," helped him up into the bus and settled him into a seat.

The bus driver started the engine, then went back to his work on the set.

Jillian covered Chase with the blanket again and another coat someone had found. Then Jillian put the makeshift cold pack on his swollen finger and had him elevate it on a foam block that was part of a prop. She didn't have any bandages, but used some masking tape to "buddy tape" his middle finger to his ring finger. It was the best that she could do with no supplies.

"Do you tolerate ibuprofen?" Jillian asked Chase.

"Yes," he said demurely.

Jillian got a tablet out from her pack and grabbed a bottled water from a case of them in front of the bus. She sat in the seat across the aisle from him and administered the medicine.

"It's going to become discolored, just so you know. And there's no two ways about it—it is going to be very sore for a while, and continue to be somewhat sore for a long time." She had known people who couldn't wear rings for years after an injury like this, and who claimed their joint hurt in certain kinds of weather, even years later.

"Jillian, thank you," Chase said. "You were right. It is better than it was, that's for sure."

"I'm glad to hear it. Now, just relax a bit and warm up."

"It'd be a lot warmer if you'd stay," he said to her.

She just looked at him. Here he was, in pain after an injury, and he still couldn't help but make a pass at her.

"Chase, I know you are not accustomed to hearing the word very often, but 'no.' I am a married woman—a very happily married woman—and you are a married man. Why don't you try figuring out what that really means for once?" she said, then walked off the bus.

The director, the assistant director, and several of the actors were in a huddle trying to figure out how to make the scene work with what they had already shot, and with only John available for the rest of the scene. John looked at Jillian as she stepped down off the bus, a concerned look on his face, and she was pretty certain that it was not *for* Chase, but *because* of Chase. She was getting pretty good at reading John. They would have to have a good talk when they got back to the lodge.

Jillian walked over to them and gave them a report. She also told them what Chase's injury would mean for him for the remainder of the shoot—his limitations, the discoloration and swelling of his hand, and that he would have to ice it often and would not be able to do certain activities with that hand. Carson Stone was beside himself, but he was thankful for her help. "How did you know how to do that?" he asked.

"Twenty-five years of nursing. By the way, when we get back, he should go to whatever clinic or hospital is nearest the lodge and have it X-rayed, just to make sure nothing is broken," she said.

He nodded his head and simply said, "Thank you for your help."

"Maybe you could include the mistake of him hitting that tank in the scene. If you captured it on film, and his painful reaction—well, you certainly couldn't get much more realistic than that," Jillian said. Suddenly realizing she may have spoken out of turn, she added, "Oh, sorry," she said, "I'm just thinking out loud."

The directors and actors talked again. "Let's see what we have," Carson said to the camera operator. She showed him.

"Hmmm, now let's try this," he said.

They shot it a few other ways, and then said they'd look at it that night and see what they could do. They also needed to decide how to tweak the script to work within the new limitations of Chase's hand.

"You could always wrap it and make it look like it's broken or cut," Jillian suggested, then stopped herself again. "I'm sorry, I'm doing it again. It's just that people often gravitate to, and have empathy for, the injured. It's like the football hero who gets hurt in the game, who has all the girls around him afterward."

"I'd assume you know how to wrap such a thing?" Carson asked.

"Definitely. Let me know if I can help in any way," she said.

"You already have. Thank you again..."

"Jillian," she said, extending her hand to Carson Stone. "Romano."

"My wife," John added proudly.

Jillian checked on Chase again in about fifteen minutes. His head was on a folded-up coat, which rested against the bus window, and he was snoring away. Injuries could do that to people—make them sleepy quickly. She removed the ice pack for the time being and suggested that someone sit on the bus with him. John seemed relieved that Jillian had not been the one to volunteer to do that.

They finished up as soon as possible, as daylight was fading fast. They cut the final scene just as the sun was setting, then packed up as quickly as they had set up and headed home on the bus. Chase temporarily woke up from his nap as everyone noisily entered the bus, all happy to be back where it was warm. They had had a tent shelter set up outside, which was helpful, but not as nice as the bus felt to all the Californians.

John and Jillian sat next to one another. John moved his leg next to hers and kept it there the entire trip. She felt like she was back in eighth grade again, sitting close to a boy on the bus and trying not to let the adult chaperones notice.

It was time for dinner when they arrived back at the lodge. A cast meeting was scheduled afterward, but then they would have time off until noon the next day. It was Sunday, and usually they would have the entire day off, but the various issues that had caused delays had put them a bit behind schedule, so noon it was.

Chase was helped off the bus, and of course, was fawned over by a group of women, as he showed them his injury. Jillian noticed Carson watching the scene. He then looked at Jillian as if to say, "I see what you mean."

The lodge arranged for Chase to be taken by one of the resort vehicles to the hospital, which was an hour away. He had some dinner first. He said he wasn't going to eat anything, but Jillian went over and talked him into it.

"You need to eat for healing. Also, when you take ibuprofen, or if they give you something even stronger when you get to the hospital, you are going to want something in your stomach," she said. "Make sure to ice your finger again, about twenty to thirty minutes, elevated above your heart."

He simply nodded affirmatively. Of course, he was right-handed and couldn't handle a fork and spoon very well. Jillian told him what was on the buffet, and they chose something that wasn't too difficult to eat one-handed. He took a seat, she filled a plate for him, and then sat it down in front of him. She brought over a cup of hot cocoa to warm him up, then turned to join John.

"Thanks, Jillian," Chase said sincerely, "for everything."

"You are welcome," she replied. She was happy that there was no innuendo this time, but noticed some women coming up to him as she was leaving and asking him if he needed any help. For whatever reason, he turned each one of them away. Jillian smiled when she saw that, and thought that there just might be hope for him yet.

Chapter Sixteen

After dinner, John and Jillian went for a walk around the property. A few people were going night skiing at a ski resort not far away, mostly those who had not been outside all afternoon. John thought that considering the way things were going, he should stay away from anything where he could possibly end up in a sling or cast, or Carson might very well have a stroke. So instead, John and Jillian opted for the safer option of a stroll on the lodge grounds.

They walked away from the bright lights of the main building, following a groomed trail. John took Jillian's gloved hand in his. They kept going until they arrived at the edge of a small frozen lake. A beautiful moon shone above and cast shadows on the hills and trees on the opposite shoreline. They stood and gazed at the sight for a minute, then John broke the silence.

"You were really something today, Jillian," John said. "You saved the day. Chase was in such agony."

"Dislocations are nasty business. They are so painful, and some people don't do very well with pain, as you obviously witnessed today. It could have been worse, though. There were no skin tears, and it didn't look like his circulation was cut off, so that's good. I just hope I did the right thing and didn't cause any damage."

"He seemed like he was doing better afterward, so I would take that as a good sign," John said, turning to her and holding her fleeced arms. "He's really something—that Chase—isn't he?"

"Oh, yes, he's *something* all right," Jillian said.

"He's interested in you, isn't he?" John asked, searching her face.

"John, I think Chase is interested in just about every female who comes into his sight," Jillian said truthfully.

"Well, there's only one female I am concerned about. I mean, everyone goes on and on about his good looks. And he's very talented. And he's young—well, forty, and by my standards, that's young..."

"John David Romano," she said, grabbing his shoulders.

"Oh-oh, now you sound like my mother when she was serious about something."

"I *am* serious about something—*you*. I think you should know me by now—the kind of woman I am, and the kind of man I'm interested in. He's the one I'm looking at right now. He is very handsome, very talented, very youthful, and most of all, he is the one I gave my heart and my solemn vow to on our wedding day."

"I was hoping you would say something like that," he said, moving closer to her.

"John, I will love you forever," she told him, and kissed him so passionately she thought the ice might begin to melt beneath them.

"Jillian," John said in a hushed tone.

She looked into his eyes, then smiled. "Last one to the room is a rotten egg," she said, and raced him back to the lodge.

The next morning, John and Jillian were dropped off by one of the lodge's SUVs in front of the main doors at 10:30 a.m., making it back just in time to eat Sunday brunch with a good majority of their group.

They walked toward the buffet table, when the actor, "Jones," called out to them.

"Where did you two go? I didn't know there was anything open before ten in the morning in this area."

"Church was open," Jillian said, smiling as they grabbed two plates off a steaming stack of them.

"You go to church?" the actor asked, surprised.

"We do," John said.

That pretty much ended the conversation, and Jones went on with his meal. Jillian noticed Chase at another table near the buffet and stopped at it for a moment. "How is the finger this morning, Chase?"

"Better. Thanks, Jillian. Nothing is broken, just sore. The Doc gave me some pain medicine to take as needed. He said you did a good job, by the way," he added.

"I'm glad to hear that," Jillian said, truly relieved. She noticed that Chase had a splint on his finger, with real medical tape, rather than the improvised job with masking tape she had crafted. She had to remember to tell Carson Stone that they really should have a first-aid kit available when they were out on location.

She filled her plate with some French toast and bacon, deciding to have something she didn't eat on a regular basis for a change. John did the same. Jillian looked around the fairly crowded room and noticed Monica sitting all by herself again. This trend was beginning to bother Jillian, and she found herself feeling sorry again for the woman.

John saw Jillian looking at Monica sitting at the table, all alone. He looked at Jillian and glanced toward Monica. "Shall we?" he asked.

"We shall," she said, smiling appreciatively at her kind husband.

Monica looked surprised, but not unhappy when they sat down. Their conversation was "small talk" primarily, but that was okay. The woman looked so unhappy, and Jillian wondered what she might do to somehow help her.

John finished his food, then Carson caught his attention and waved him over to his table. "Excuse me a moment," he said to Jillian and Monica.

When John was out of earshot, Monica quietly said, "He doesn't love me anymore."

Jillian didn't know what to say. She wasn't completely certain who the "he" was in Monica's sentence—Monica's husband—or hers.

Monica must have sensed Jillian's confusion. "My husband, Ben. He doesn't love me anymore."

"Are you sure?"

"I only know he's never around. He doesn't call me when we're apart, and he doesn't talk to me when we're together. I don't know what he's thinking. All he does is work," she said.

The words reminded her so much of Karen and Robert's former situation, and she shared their story briefly as well as the story she had told Karen about her own parents. Karen had used Jillian's mother's tactics to get Robert's attention, and it had started an entire new chapter in their marriage.

"Why don't you try it? Pick a place you know he loves to go, somewhere that is special to you both, or to your entire family. Tell Ben, or Ben and the boys, that you already have reservations, and you are going with or without him or them, and see what happens. What do you have to lose at this point?"

Monica sat quietly, considering the idea. "I'll think about it," she said finally.

Just then John returned. He looked at his watch. "I guess it's time to get going," he said.

Jillian stood up to join him, and they picked up their trays.

"See you in a bit," John said to Monica.

Monica nodded, deep in thought.

That afternoon, Jillian received a call from Marty. Jillian was in the middle of writing a chapter in her new book when the call came in.

"Mom!" Marty exclaimed. "What is going on up there?"

"What do you mean?" Jillian asked.

"The Internet gossip sites and magazines are all saying that you and Dad are breaking up—that Dad and Monica are back together—and that you are having an affair with Chase Cheekwood! There are even photos of Dad and Monica sitting together at a table, and you holding Chase's hand."

"What! I mean, Dad did sit with Monica. I purposely left him sitting with her the other day so she could apologize to him—which she did. And yesterday, I helped put Chase's dislocated finger back in its proper place, then examined it, but that is the only time I touched his hand. Where are they getting these photos?"

She remembered earlier, during the filming in Los Angeles, that there were photos of Monica and John, coming out of the studio or in a scene, and she had thought maybe it was someone on the set. Whoever it was had to have been at the scene yesterday. She was going to warn John and start watching at the next opportunity for anyone who might be taking pictures. It would have to be done with a phone, she thought, or else it would have been too obvious.

"I don't know, Mom, but it's not good. I was pretty sure that it was all nonsense, but I thought you would want to know what people are saying, and that there will be those who actually believe it."

"Yes, perhaps I should write about it in my blog. What do you think?"

"It wouldn't be a bad idea. Your readers won't want to take

advice from someone who is cheating on her husband—or who they think is cheating—so you will want to clear that up as soon as possible."

They hung up. *This is getting serious.* Jillian called her agent, then posted the "real story" in her blog. *What's happening, Lord?*

After doing some damage control, Jillian decided to watch the scene John and the others were working on out in the makeshift studio. She didn't want to make any noise, so she crept into the room. She stopped when she noticed Jones, the actor who had remarked about her and John going to church that morning, holding a phone up and apparently taking a photo. She looked at his subjects—John and Monica. John had his arm on her shoulder, as they were just finishing a scene where they had hugged. Jillian watched Jones as he took a few more quick shots, looked around, and then put the phone away quickly in his pocket.

The director called for a ten-minute break. Jillian didn't know if she should tell John what was going on, but when he came over to her, he could tell by her expression that there was a problem.

The first thing he asked her was, "What's wrong?"

She told him about the call from Marty, the online and magazine gossip, and what she had just seen. He said that he should tell Carson before things got even worse.

John walked over to the director and filled him in. Carson put his hands to his head as if to say, "What next?"

He called Jones over and asked him if he could see his phone. The actor wouldn't let him touch it. Carson told him that either he handed it over or he was done, right then and there. If he had nothing to hide, then there wouldn't be a problem.

The actor gave him the phone reluctantly. After a minute, Carson turned to him and asked, "Why are you doing this?"

Kathy J. Jacobson

"I needed the money," he said, looking at the ground.

"What is it? Drugs?" he asked.

He hesitated. "Gambling," he said, his eyes filling with tears.

"Here's your phone. You're fired," Carson said. "And if any more of these photos, like the ones you just took, show up anywhere, I'll see you in court—and I'll make sure you'll never work in Hollywood again."

Jones took the phone and began gathering his things.

John looked at Jillian, who had watched the entire thing, and felt pretty bad about the situation.

"Carson," John said. "Isn't there some way we can work this out?"

"You want me to keep that man on the set—who is trying to ruin your life and others' with those photos?" Carson asked in disbelief.

"I'm not happy about it, but it sounds like he is someone who needs help. Maybe we could get him some, especially if he were to come forward with the story behind all those photos. That way, his life and career aren't ruined, and hopefully everyone else's reputations can be cleared, too."

"You really want me to do that?" Carson asked.

"Yes, I do. I know how it feels to have an addiction, and it isn't fun," John said, referring to his past problems with painkillers. John had now been in recovery for more than twenty years, but he never forgot his early struggles.

"Jones!" Carson called out to the actor who was heading toward the door. "Come back here a minute, please."

The man, head still hanging, walked over, his coat and backpack in his hand.

"Romano here wants you to stay on the job. But there are some conditions I have for you. One, you are going to get treatment for this problem of yours as soon as we are back in L.A. Secondly, you are going to give the press the story behind all those photos you've been sharing and why. And third, you are going to give that phone to my assistant, who is going to delete every one of those photos. Do you think you can do that?"

"I don't have money for treatment," he said.

"We'll figure something out," Carson told him, and John nodded.

"Okay, I agree. Thank you—both—so much," he said, and handed over his phone to the assistant director, who was wearily standing nearby to see how the situation would play out.

"Now, let's get back to work! If we ever get this movie finished, it will be a miracle!" Carson barked. "Places, everyone!"

Jones looked at John, then extended his hand to him to shake. "I'm sorry, Mr. Romano," he said.

"You are forgiven," John replied. "Just get some help."

The man nodded, and they got back to work.

Jillian had watched the entire scene play out. She stood on the sidelines, so incredibly proud of her husband, and with a heart so full that it felt like it was going to burst. *What a good man you are, John D. Romano.*

Chapter Seventeen

Miraculously, the next few days of filming went without a hitch. Carson Stone was so happy that he hired a live band for a dance in the dining hall at the lodge, following the meal on their final night in Alaska. They had a marvelous dinner that included many types of local fish and game. Carson sat at the head table, playing the role of master of ceremonies and making many toasts throughout the evening. He was very relieved that things had worked out in the end, even with all the incidents along the way. In fact, he said some things may have worked out even better than he had originally planned.

Jillian got up to get a glass of water and ran into Monica at the back of the dining room. They stood together and talked for a moment as the band played its first song. Jillian didn't know if she should ask Monica about Ben, but she didn't have to.

Monica's face looked different—hopeful. "I did it, Jillian. I did what you suggested. I called Ben, and then each of the boys. I told them I made reservations at our favorite resort, where we have had many happy times together. I told them the dates and that there were tickets on hold for them. Then I told them that I was going—with or without them."

Monica paused. Jillian wasn't sure if that was a good thing, or bad.

"They are coming, Jillian. I can't believe it. Ben and I talked—for the first time in a very long time. He wants to talk some more. And the boys...I can't even remember the last time we were all together. Thank you for your help," she said sincerely, her voice filled with emotion.

Just then, the band began playing its next song, and they watched as some of the people began to dance. Others still sat at the tables conversing. John was one of them, talking and laughing away, sitting next to the actor, Jones, and unbelievably, Chase Cheekwood, who was sitting where Jillian had been seated minutes before. It was an amazing sight. John looked over their way, and his eyes met Jillian's. He gave her one of those looks and smiles that made her feel like they were the only two people in the world.

"I'm so happy for you, Monica. Now please excuse me. I think I have to dance with my husband," she said.

"John dances?" she asked incredulously. She shook her head. "If he had been that much fun when we were together, I would never have broken up with him," Monica quipped.

"Well, I'm sure glad you did, Monica," Jillian said sincerely.

Monica chuckled slightly. "You are good for him, Jillian. I've never seen John so happy."

"I'm glad to hear that, because he sure is good for me, and I've never been so happy."

Monica smiled at her, and she smiled back. Then Jillian found herself hugging the woman, much to Monica's surprise. It was clear that Monica wasn't accustomed to people hugging her, but after the shock wore off, she hugged Jillian back.

"I'll keep on praying for you and your family," Jillian said to her quietly.

"Thank you," she said, looking like she was thinking about that bit of information.

Jillian looked at John again, and each of them began walking toward the dance floor. They met on the parqueted wooden surface, their eyes never leaving the other's, and seemed to melt into each other's arms. Jillian had to fight the urge to kiss him, and she was pretty sure that he was having the same internal struggle as they began to sway together to the music.

"Do you know what Carson told me this evening?" John finally asked, breaking the silence.

She shook her head "no."

"He said he should have put you on the payroll." John grinned that huge grin of his.

"Did he now?" she asked, looking into his eyes, which were dancing themselves.

"Everything was a mess before you got up here, especially between Monica and me. And now you've got us eating at the same table and talking to each other like human beings. And just a moment ago, you and she were hugging each other," he said in amazement. "How did you do that?"

"It was like this," she said, hugging him to her body.

He shook his head and laughed, then he hugged her back, pulling her even closer.

He continued to pierce her soul with his eyes. The song ended and they just stood there. The band began another slow song, so they began to move with the music again.

"And what if you hadn't been there when Chase got hurt? Or what if you hadn't found out who was taking those photos?" he went on.

"I was blessed to be in the right place at the right time," she said.

"I know that feeling," he said, tightening his grip on her hand and her waist. He looked like he just might break down and kiss her when they were interrupted by none other than Chase Cheekwood.

"May I cut in?" he asked.

They both looked at him at the same time, and in unison said, "Not a chance."

He smiled. "I didn't think so, but it was worth a try. I think I'll go call my wife," he said, sounding like he was thinking out loud. They watched him walk toward the door to the lobby, pulling out his phone.

John and Jillian smiled at one another. Jillian took her hand that was on John's shoulder and put it to his cheek.

"Maybe we could continue this dance somewhere else?" she whispered to him.

He nodded and took her hand, and they exited the dance floor.

The next morning everyone headed to the airport on the rented bus. It had been quite an adventure from the very start—and it wasn't over yet.

Jillian went up to the counter at the small airport to check in.

"I'm sorry, ma'am," the man behind the counter said. "We're overbooked." You'll have to wait until tonight, and that's not even for sure. It might be tomorrow."

Shocked, she asked, "How did that happen?" She was not at all happy about the thought of being on another last flight of the day, and even worse, flying again without John. She went over to John and told him what was going on.

He became quite agitated and spoke loudly. "If you're not going, I'm not going," he said.

"But honey, don't you have an audition tomorrow afternoon?" she asked.

"I don't care about any audition. I don't want you flying on this airline without me. If anything...if anything were to ever happen...

I'd want to be with you. I'd want us to be together." John was holding onto her arms and getting quite visibly upset. He was catching the attention of others around them, including Monica.

Jillian held him, trying to reassure him that it would be okay, but he couldn't be convinced.

"I'll change my ticket to go with you," he said, and turned toward the counter.

"You don't have to," a voice said. It was Monica, who was just coming from the ticket counter. "I just arranged for Jillian to have my ticket. I'll go on the later flight, or even tomorrow. I'm not in any rush."

John looked at her, absolutely stunned, then threw his arms around her. "Thank you, Monica. Thank you so very much," he said, and pulled back, still in disbelief. Monica looked equally surprised by John's hug, which wasn't an act this time.

Monica and Jillian went over to the ticket counter and made the final changes, just to make sure all was in order and to get their new boarding passes for both the flight from Valdez to Anchorage, and then from Anchorage to Los Angeles. Now it was Jillian's turn to give Monica a hug.

Just then, they heard the boarding call. John and Jillian's row was announced, and they headed to the walkway. They turned around one last time and waved to Monica, who stood with a huge smile on her face for the first time in a very long while.

John and Jillian took their seats on the plane. Jillian put her bag under the seat in front of her, and they buckled their seat belts— tightly.

"What just happened?" John asked, still dazed.

"New creation," Jillian said, putting her head on his shoulder, and feeling very thankful.

It had never felt so wonderful to be home. The short time in Alaska had seemed like a lifetime, and now it was time to get back to business as usual.

Already the true story behind the photos by Jones was circulating on the Internet, and soon an article would appear in a popular magazine. Jillian's blog followers had been very supportive and understanding from the start. Many of them had been following her for over a year and knew better than to believe the gossip magazines, both print and online.

Jillian's agent was none too happy, but she also knew that sometimes even bad publicity could work to one's advantage, if it didn't get too out of control. None of the bookstores or other places where Jillian was scheduled to go seemed too concerned, with the exception of one church, which wanted to know more about the allegations. After they were given more information, they kept Jillian as a speaker.

Jillian was relieved about the fairly quick resolution of the problem, not only for her sake but because of the Academy Award ceremony, which was only a week away. She didn't want anything to spoil John's special night.

Jillian was meeting that evening with Marianna for the fitting of the dress. She couldn't wait to see it. She remembered to call and tell Marianna about the new intercom system. The front yard fence and gate project had been completed while they were gone. It was perfect timing, after all the publicity of the last week and the Oscars coming up. John and Jillian felt saddened, but very relieved that it was in place.

John was still gone at his audition when Marianna came over. If the audition hadn't been for a movie that sounded quite in-

Kathy J. Jacobson

triguing, he would not have considered auditioning the day after returning home from Alaska.

Jillian was actually glad that he wasn't home, however, as she wanted her dress to be a surprise. John had bought a brand new tuxedo and dress shoes, and she couldn't wait to see him in them.

Marianna arrived at 6:30 p.m., carrying the dress in a long protective bag draped over her arms. Jillian wondered how the petite woman could even ring the doorbell, she was so encumbered.

They used the living room this time for the fitting, as there was better and brighter artificial lighting in the room. Jillian made certain the blinds were completely closed, and then stepped up onto a stool in her new shoes. Marianna showed her the best way to get into the dress on her own, as Jillian wanted to dress by herself that evening. Marianna also brought jewelry she had chosen to go with the dress. The young woman was very talented, and Jillian trusted her judgment completely, so she had asked her to choose the accessories. She even had a beautiful hairpin that matched the gown. Jillian would have never thought of something like that on her own.

Jillian had never worn anything so amazing in her life. The gold material shimmered, yet the design was very simple and elegant. It was strapless, with a gentle twist of material down the front of the gown. Marianna helped her with undergarment tips. The young woman had thought of everything.

"Marianna, I hope you understand that you have a real gift from God," Jillian said.

Even with her darker complexion, Jillian noticed the young woman blush.

"You are too kind, Ms. Jillian," she said. Jillian still couldn't get her to call her just by her first name.

"No, it's the truth. So, what do I owe you, Marianna?" Jillian asked.

Marianna told her how much the jewelry and material cost, and that was all she cared about getting back before her credit card bill came.

"It is such an honor to have made a gown for the Oscars, and for you," Marianna said.

Jillian took out her checkbook. There was no way she was only going to pay this young woman for the jewelry and material. She knew what some of the dresses and accessories for the Oscars were going for down on Rodeo Drive, or commissioned from a famous designer.

Jillian made out a check to her, and then gave her a hug. She promised to have her picture taken in the gown and would make certain that Marianna would be credited for the design.

Jillian saw her to the door and thanked her again. Marianna had not looked at the amount on the check when Jillian handed it to her. It was still a bargain compared to Beverly Hills, but Jillian had also made it well worth Marianna's time, of which she had little between her work and school commitments.

Jillian was just turning away from the door when she heard Marianna exclaim loudly, "Dios mio!" She had most likely looked at her check. Jillian smiled on her way up the stairs to hang up the dress where John wouldn't see it until the special night.

The next day, Jillian and John were invited to Karen and Robert's for dinner. Jillian was looking forward to seeing her friends. Jillian made some cookies that morning to take along for Rick. She and John really enjoyed the intelligent and sensitive boy. She was often amazed that he was doing so well, considering the parenting—if one could call it that—which he had endured for most of his life. Perhaps he inherited his mother's disposition. But Jil-

Kathy J. Jacobson

lian still worried that somehow, someday, some of Rick's father's qualities would emerge.

Jillian was very happy that Karen and Robert were taking him to a therapist to help him through this transition time as a foster child, and as a child who just lost his only living parent. She was really impressed with the dedication and care her friends were showing Rick. If he couldn't make it in their home, he wouldn't make it anywhere.

They sat around the large oval dinner table. Rick had helped Karen make enchiladas for dinner, and they were fabulous. They had gone online to find a recipe, as neither of them had ever made them, but it was one of Rick's favorite foods, other than pancakes. A salad, rice and beans, flour tortillas, and flan filled out the menu.

As dessert was served, Robert, Karen, and Rick made an announcement. Karen and Robert had filed paperwork for adoption.

"Wonderful! Congratulations," John said, and put his hand on Rick's shoulder to congratulate him.

"I am so happy for you all," Jillian said, then turning to Rick, she added, "Welcome to the club."

"Club?" he asked.

"Yes, of those of us who are adopted."

"You're adopted?" he asked, his eyes wide as saucers.

Jillian nodded her head.

"You are?" Karen sounded just as surprised.

Jillian thought perhaps she had once mentioned it to Karen, but it didn't always come up in the course of normal conversation.

"The way you talked about your mother, I thought..." Karen didn't finish the sentence.

"You will find that one doesn't have to *give birth* to be a real mom," Jillian replied. "I couldn't have asked for better parents."

"What's it like to be adopted?" Rick asked.

"It's the best," she said. "Your parents choose to be your parents, and pick you to be their child. That's pretty cool."

"Yeah, I guess that is," Rick said thoughtfully.

"This calls for a toast," said Robert. They lifted their glasses and clinked them together.

"Cheers—to adoption!" John said, and they all followed suit.

That night, Jillian laid in bed with her head on John's chest as he rubbed her shoulder gently. He did that often when he was thinking.

"What are you thinking about, John?" Jillian asked.

"Adoption," he said, taking her completely by surprise.

She wasn't sure how to respond to that statement. She wondered if he was thinking that perhaps they should consider adopting a child like Karen and Robert were doing. She was quiet a moment. Finally she asked, "What about adoption?"

"I was wondering if Marty would consider becoming my legal daughter. I would like to adopt her," he said, like it was just an ordinary point of conversation.

Jillian was stunned. She sat up, turned on the lamp next to the bed, and looked at him, tears forming in her eyes. This pronouncement was one of the nicest things she had ever heard anyone say regarding her daughter, and she had heard many good ones.

John continued, "What do you think of that idea, Jillian?"

She felt very emotional at that particular moment and couldn't speak. Instead, she just stroked his face with her hand, as a tear rolled down her cheek. Finally, the words came. "I think you are the most wonderful husband—and father—ever," she said softly.

John brushed away her tear. "I love you, Jillian, and Marty is a part of you. I know she didn't come *from* both of us, but somehow

I feel that maybe she was created *for* both of us."

If John said one more word, Jillian was going lose it completely. She had never loved anyone in this world as much as she loved him at that moment. All she could do was nod her head in agreement.

"I'll ask her tomorrow," he said, then pulled her into his embrace.

The next morning, John flew to San Francisco and rented a car. He had called Marty early in the morning and asked if he could take her out to lunch—a date—just the two of them this time. He had told her he had something important to ask her.

Luckily, Marty had two more days before she began her classes. She had a few things to get at the bookstore, but that was it. She could get them the next day.

Marty sat in the restaurant at Fisherman's Wharf and waited for John to arrive. Her friend had loaned her a car for the day, which made things a lot easier. She wondered what John was up to. She figured he must be in town for an audition or meeting of some sort, and wanted to know something about her mom. Maybe he was already looking ahead to the next month, when they would have their first anniversary. She could barely believe it had almost been an entire year since they all became a family. It was one of the happiest days of Marty's life, and definitely of her mother's life. She had never seen her mom as happy as she had been since she married John, and she would adore him forever for that.

She almost didn't recognize John at first when he came through the restaurant door in a Giants baseball cap, sunglasses, and a black leather jacket. Then she remembered that he was up for an Academy Award and he was a celebrity. She didn't really think of him that way, since at home he was just a regular person who grilled burgers and made her mom laugh. She and Michael were going to his movie that night at a cinema that was featuring all the movies that were nominated for best picture or who had anyone in them up for awards on Sunday night. They had been watching for John's movie since they arrived in Stanford.

John looked around, and once Marty figured out who he was, she waved him over. His face spread into his usual, huge grin. Her mother had once told her that his grin was one of her favorite things about John, and Marty could understand why.

She stood up, and they hugged each other, then sat back down. They were seated in a booth in the back of the restaurant, which is what John requested she try to reserve for them if at all possible, since it was more private.

"So, Dad, do you have an audition or something up here today?" Marty asked after they settled into their seats.

"No, I just wanted to see you," he said.

"Really?" Marty asked.

"Really. I have a question for you, but I suppose that we should look at the menu first and order. I'm starving. How about you?"

"Me, too, but I'm always hungry. High metabolism, and I think my body's still trying to catch up from my bout of Dengue," she said, shivering at the thought of the nasty fever she had contracted shortly after her mom and dad had visited her in Senegal. It was the worst experience of her life. She still kept telling herself that all was relative, however. It could have been Ebola, and she could be no longer living. Knowing those were real possibilities had kept her more positive on the days when she was still dealing with the "fallout" from Dengue fever.

John nodded in agreement. "I'm sure it will take a while to be one hundred percent after an ordeal like that," he said, shuddering at the thought of the huge scare he and Jillian had faced when they had received a call saying Marty had been put into isolation at the hospital.

"Let's forget about that right now. I don't want to spoil my lunch," she said, and John agreed wholeheartedly.

They both ordered crab salad with sourdough bread on the side. They laughed when they both asked for the same thing. The waiter left with the menus, and Marty looked at John.

"Are you sure we're not really related?" Marty asked jokingly.

"Well, I'm pretty sure not biologically, but that brings me to the reason I flew up here today," he said.

Marty looked at him inquisitively.

"I have a question for you, Marty. You don't have to give me an answer immediately—I would understand if you want some time to think about this."

Now she was really intrigued. She thought this was a question about an anniversary gift, or maybe something to do with Oscar night.

John cleared his throat and looked her straight in the eyes. "I know I'm not your biological father, Marty, but I love you as if I were. I want to be your dad in every way that I can be, including being your legal one. I am wondering if you might consider letting me adopt you as my own daughter? You don't have to change your name or anything, unless you would like to, but I would really like to be your father."

Marty was one of those people who rarely cried. She was always proud of her ability to control her emotions, and found it very helpful in the healthcare profession, but tears began streaming down her face as John spoke. For all but the last year of her life, she had felt she had no father in the world, or at least no one who wished to be claimed as such. Even though her mom was the most amazing person she had ever known, and had done a fantastic job of raising her and making her feel loved, there was always this nagging feeling in the back of her heart, that her father didn't want her. Now, here was John, who flew all the way up to San Francisco during one of the craziest weeks of his life, to ask her to be his daughter. She was completely floored—in a good way.

John took her hands in his. "Like I said, you don't have to answer…"

"I want to be your daughter—in every way possible. Yes, you may adopt me. I would be honored to be yours," she said.

Now it was John who looked like he might lose it, but the two of them pulled themselves together just in time for their food to arrive at the table. They lifted their glasses of raspberry lemonade in a toast.

"To my daughter," John said as his glass touched Marty's. Then he gave her another one of his award-winning grins.

"To my dad," Marty said, with a brilliant smile to match.

John decided to stay that evening and go to the movie with Michael and Marty. He thought it would be fun in an odd sort of way. He had called Jerry and was going to stay at his house afterward, then fly back home the next morning from San Francisco. Jerry said he would go with them to the movie, too, if he could get out of his meeting on time.

The four of them caught a quick fast-food dinner, then walked into the cinema early before most of the others arrived. John wore his hat and glasses to the show, until the lights went down in the cinema for the previews to begin. John rarely watched his movies at a theater. Of course, he had gone to the premiere of this one with Jillian. He had enjoyed that, but only because she was with him. He didn't always like to see himself on the screen, and often found himself critiquing rather than watching a film.

On this night, however, he was celebrating. He sat with Marty on one side and Jerry on the other. For once, he just let himself

Kathy J. Jacobson

relax and enjoy the movie. He tried to pretend he was watching people he didn't know, and that he didn't know every line and every little thing that had gone wrong trying to film a particular scene. It was fun to hear people laughing where they were supposed to laugh, make a frightened noise in a suspenseful moment, and sniff when they were supposed to be sad.

John was so caught up in being one of the audience members that he didn't put his hat and glasses on as they walked out of the theater. They stood in the lobby for a moment, putting on their jackets.

One woman next to them turned to John and said, "Did you know that you look a lot like that actor who played Mack?"

"I do?" John asked. "That's a good thing, I hope?"

"Oh, yes. He's a hottie," she said matter-of-factly, and then walked out with her date, who looked perturbed at her remark.

John quickly put back on the Giants cap he had bought at the airport.

"We had better get you out of here, you 'hottie,'" Marty said, giggling.

They all went back to Jerry's for a while, having some tea and coffee. Marty and Michael walked back to the medical student housing which was not far from his house. It was a cool, but calm night, so they said they didn't mind walking such a short distance. John shook hands with Michael, and he and his soon-to-be daughter in every way hugged and kissed each other goodbye.

Jerry and John stayed up and talked for another hour. Jerry was missing Carol so much he could hardly stand it. John remembered well the forty days between his proposal and his marriage, and that was bad enough. He at least got to see Jillian every day, whereas Jerry and Carol were two thousand miles apart.

The only positive was that Jerry was very busy. He was attempting to clean up his property to sell it, teaching, and getting his retirement papers in order. Carol was doing the same on her end. The two newlyweds talked on the phone twice every day and texted each other like teenagers.

"I never thought I could be so in love," Jerry said.

"I know exactly what you are talking about, friend. It's wonderful, isn't it?" John replied.

"It is. I just hope I can sell this house soon so we can move to Los Angeles after the semester is over. The house needs a bit of updating. After my first wife died, I just didn't care about it, or anything anymore, but now I realize I should have been taking better care of things," Jerry said.

John completely understood what it felt like to drop out of the world. He had done the same thing for two years.

"You would think with it being only a mile from the medical school..." John stopped mid-sentence. All of a sudden, he got an idea and spent the next half an hour discussing it with Jerry. He couldn't wait to get home the next day and talk it over with Jillian.

Chapter Eighteen

It had been a long night without John at her side. Sometimes Jillian could barely believe she had spent almost the entirety of her life sleeping alone. Now, even one night without her husband seemed painful.

The previous afternoon, Marty had called and told her about her lunch date with John. They had both cried, which was a rarity, but then again, it was a rare situation, to say the least. Marty informed Jillian that she wanted to change her last name to Johnson Romano, just as Jillian had upon her marriage. Jillian knew that John would be thrilled to hear that when he got home.

Jillian had looked at the clock for about the hundredth time that day when she heard John coming in the front door. He had taken a taxi from the airport so that she didn't have to spend half of her day picking him up. For as little as she had written, she may as well have spent the time playing chauffeur. She just could not concentrate with all the things that were going on.

She ran to the foyer, where he was just putting down his small bag. He looked up at her, and there was that fabulous grin again.

"I'm going to be a father," he said, extending his arms to her.

"Congratulations, Dad," she said as she was enveloped in his embrace.

John kissed the top of her head and held her for a long moment.

"I thought getting an Academy Award nomination was a great moment, but yesterday was even better," he said sincerely.

Jillian looked at him and just shook her head. "I don't know what's going to happen on Sunday night, John, but you sure are a winner in my book."

He smiled, then kissed her tenderly.

Later John discussed the idea with Jillian that he and Jerry had tossed around the night before. John thought that he and Jillian should buy Jerry's house in its current condition. Jerry really didn't have the time or the money to fix it up. They could then proceed with a few different options. One would be to fix it up and try to sell it to a doctor or professor who would like to live close to campus. Or they could leave it "as is" and rent it out to medical students. The third option was to donate it to the university as housing for temporary medical school project interns in global health, like Marty. Of course, she would be done and gone by the time Jerry moved out, but there would be many others coming and going for years to come after her.

"Why don't we look into option number three?" Jillian said with a smile. "We could ask Drew about how to best proceed with that. It seems like it would be most in keeping with our future goals of helping others."

"I thought that would be your first choice, but I didn't want to speak for you. Let's get the ball rolling on that, and I will tell Jerry that he doesn't have to put the house on the market. It will save him a lot of headache. He and Carol can buy something here, too, if we buy his house now. It seems it would be a win-win situation for everyone," he said. "I need to touch base with Drew anyway, over the final details we need done for the acting school. It will be a great anniversary gift to have it up and running."

Jillian nodded, so proud of her husband for the generous person he was. Buying the house would help Jerry tremendously, and it would benefit future medical students in the global health field. Jillian could only imagine how happy Carol was going to be when she heard the news. Now she and Jerry could find a home in Los Angeles, and they could all be together this summer, Jillian hoped. As if her life wasn't already fantastic, now her best friend from Madison would be living nearby. Her dream-come-true life just kept getting better and better.

Jillian laid in bed that night, cradled in John's arms. She said a prayer of thanks for all the incredible things that had happened in the past two days. There wasn't just one, but two, adoptions in the works. And now with this house deal plan, they would be helping friends while at the same time helping others they wouldn't even know, who would in turn help many suffering people around the world in the future. It was truly, as John had said, a "win-win" situation.

Jillian had commitments on Saturday, but had been relieved of the ones for Sunday due to the Academy Award ceremony. She and John went to the early service at church that morning. People couldn't believe he was there on the day of the Academy Awards. John and Jillian, however, thought it was the perfect place to be, as they both felt so incredibly thankful for the past year.

The sermon was based on Matthew Chapter 6—that one cannot serve both God and wealth, and not to trust in or put too much emphasis on things that were just temporary but to seek first the kingdom of God. It seemed very appropriate on that day. As much as Jillian would love to see John win an award, she also knew that there were things that were so much more important in life, and she could sense that he came away from the service with a similar feeling.

Many people wished him good luck on the way out of church. Buck and Nancy were back from their honeymoon, arriving home a few days before. Jillian thought her friends were absolutely glowing with happiness. Jillian wondered if the couple would continue to go to Grace in the future. The last she knew, they hadn't figured out the permanent housing arrangements quite yet. Nancy still had her house, which she had lived in since her children were babies. Buck had his huge ranch northeast of Los Angeles. It wouldn't be an easy decision as to how to proceed. Jillian would pray for her friends on that one.

As they left the building, Buck and Nancy asked them if they wanted to go out for lunch. They thought that would not be a wise decision on this day. Then Nancy suggested that they go to her house. She had made a pot of chicken soup the day before, having never mastered cooking for one—or now two. Jillian had had this soup once before, on the weekend when John had fired her. They accepted and met up at Nancy's house.

Nancy's house was a split-level ranch with four bedrooms. Her six kids had occupied three of them, while she and her husband, and later just she, had occupied the fourth. It was a pleasant home, and while it needed some updates, it had received meticulous care over the years. There wasn't a speck of dust to be found in the entire house, and the cabinetry and floors gleamed.

The four enjoyed the tasty soup, along with bread that Nancy had made in a bread machine early that morning, and a fresh fruit salad. Both John and Jillian were grateful for the meal—comfort food on a stressful day—and the conversation.

John and Jillian told them about John's plans to adopt Marty.

Nancy and Buck talked about their trip, which had been a cruise off the western coast of Mexico. They loved the food, the people, and especially the Mayan ruins. Nancy showed off a beautiful silver necklace Buck had bought for her, and he then showed them a gleaming silver belt buckle she had gotten for him.

The two were clearly in love, but there was still tension in the air about the house situation. Jillian decided to help Nancy put things away in the kitchen, purposely leaving John and Buck together to talk.

The two men got up and walked out to the patio overlooking the backyard. A swing set was still standing in the yard from when Nancy's children were little. The grandkids now enjoyed playing on it.

Buck sighed as they stood outside.

"I know this is a nice house," he said. "It's just…"

John was patient and let him think about what he wanted to say.

Buck turned to him. "I just feel like it's not *my* house—or *our* house. It's the house Nancy bought with 'er first husband. I know Ed was a good guy and all, but it still bothers me. I guess I shouldn't feel that way, but I do."

"I get that," John said.

"Y'all do?" Buck asked, surprised.

"Certainly."

"I wouldn't mind having a spot here in town," town being Buck's description of Los Angeles. "I just don't want this spot. And I don't think we need a house with four bedrooms. If the grandkids want to visit, they can come to the ranch. There's tons of room out there," he said.

"Have you told Nancy all this?" John asked.

"Nah. I just can't seem to get the words out of my mouth," he said. "I don't want to hurt 'er feelin's and all."

"I think it would hurt her more to know that you couldn't tell her what you are thinking. Honesty is usually the best policy in a relationship," John said.

"I suppose. Y'all think I really should tell 'er, huh?" Buck asked.

"Yes, I do," John said.

"Okay, I believe y'all. Y'all seem to have a good relationship, so I trust y'all."

"Thanks, Buck. I think we have a great relationship," John said, smiling.

Just then they were joined by their wives. They all sat down on the chairs for a bit, but then Jillian said that they should really get going, as they were on a strict timeline. A limo was picking them up at the house in a few hours, and they would be off to Oscars.

"I've been praying for you, John," Nancy announced, putting her hand on his arm.

"Thank you, Nancy," he said, and bent down to give her a hug. "And thank you for the delicious soup, too. It was just what the doctor ordered today," he said, grinning down at her.

"Buck, nice to see you," John added, turning to the tall man and shaking his hand, then giving him a little wink that only Jillian noticed.

Jillian hugged them both, and then they were off to the Land Rover.

"So, what was the little wink about?" Jillian asked as they got to the car.

"You noticed that, did you?" he said, opening the car door for her. "I just gave Buck a little advice—to tell his wife what was on his mind."

"You did, did you?" she asked, as he climbed in next to her and buckled up.

"I told him it's a good practice to do that."

"Agreed. Okay, so what's on *your* mind?" she asked him. She was teasing him, certain that he could only be thinking of one thing—

Kathy J. Jacobson

the awards ceremony in just a few hours.

"I was wishing I didn't have to go to the Oscars. I'd rather do this," he said, and leaned over to kiss her.

Jillian jumped through the shower and started in on her hair and makeup, which would take double the normal time. Her hair dresser taught her how to do her hair, and another person at the salon had given her makeup lessons. Marianna had told her what shades of eye shadow would look best with her eyes and the dress.

She followed Marianna's instructions for putting on her dress, and miraculously, it worked. She had been sure that she wouldn't be able to maneuver the zipper, but she did.

John was showering and dressing in another bedroom. They were meeting in the foyer, where they would wait for the intercom to buzz and the limo to arrive at their door. There had already been paparazzi lined up on the street when they came home from Buck and Nancy's. She was certain that they would follow them all the way to the Dolby Theatre.

John arrived in the foyer first. Jillian slowly made it down the curved steps, feeling like she was in some kind of movie as she held onto the rail. John didn't hear her at first, but then glanced up.

His eyes widened, then he looked at her the way he had looked at her the night in Italy when she wore the dress she had bought in Rome.

"How am I supposed to concentrate on anything tonight when you look like this?"

"Thank you. I'll take that as a compliment. I might ask you the same question," she said sincerely. The new tuxedo had been a good buy, and it fit him to a T.

He looked deeply into her eyes and looked like he was about

to kiss her. Just then the intercom buzzed. "Saved by the buzzer," John said softly. He kissed her hand, then walked over to push the button to let the driver into the gate.

Jillian had never been in a theater with 3,400 seats before. Because John was a nominee, their seats would be on the main floor, center section. She had made it through the toughest part of the evening already, the red carpet arrival. John had held her arm proudly as the camera flashes nearly blinded them. She had been instructed how to hold her head so that they wouldn't bother her as much, and it seemed to help—a little.

After they got inside, John had to stop for photos and brief interviews, of course. Jillian didn't mind. She was loving each and every moment, watching him get the recognition he so richly deserved. A few people asked if they could photograph her. One asked her who made her "stunning" gown. She thought Marianna would be proud that this term had been applied to the gown twice already that evening.

Jillian answered, "Marianna," like she was a commonly known designer. Another woman asked her for contact information for Marianna, and she gladly gave her the number on the business card Marianna had just had printed.

Several other wives and dates of those up for awards stood together, some sipping champagne. Jillian had never really cared for "bubbly," so she simply had a glass of water. She didn't really know anyone around her at that moment, so she was happy when Carson Stone came through the doorway. He was nominated—again—for Best Director, for the film he had made prior to the pipeline movie with John and Monica.

"Jillian!" he said, approaching her. Those around her began paying attention to her in a new way since Carson Stone had ac-

Kathy J. Jacobson

knowledged her. He held out his hand to her. She put hers out toward his, and for the second time in an evening, someone kissed her hand. She felt like she was a "royal" with this kind of treatment.

"You look stunning, my dear," he said.

She smiled at the word, hearing it yet again, and planned to give Marianna a full report before the night was over.

"You are too kind, Mr. Stone. How are you?"

"Call me Carson. I am very well, thank you. I have enjoyed my two-week break, but now I am ready for my next adventure. Something very intriguing just came across my desk yesterday. I was just about to call you and your husband about it, and I may have an interesting proposition for both of you. Perhaps we could meet sometime this week?"

Jillian hardly knew what to say. She was not used to award-nominated movie directors having a proposition that included her—her husband certainly but not her.

"I think that could be arranged. After this week, I am gone for two weeks on a book tour."

"Yes, I read about your book and blog. Very interesting. I'm going to buy a copy for myself, and another for a good friend of mine who just suffered the end of a long-term relationship and is taking it quite poorly. Maybe I could have you autograph them when we have our meeting?"

"Of course," she said. Jillian again felt like she was in a dream. Now she had a famous movie director asking for *her* autograph.

John joined them at that moment, and the two men shook hands vigorously.

"I was just telling your lovely wife that I would like to talk to both of you sometime this week, if you are available," Carson said.

"I believe that could happen," John replied, with a look that matched Jillian's just moments before. He, too, was a bit surprised by both of them being invited to speak with Carson.

Just then they were called to be escorted to their seats.

Carson turned to John and asked, "So, John, are you ready to accept your first statue?"

"I would have to win one first, Carson," John said.

"If you don't win, the Academy has really gone to the dogs," he replied bluntly.

"Thank you for your vote of confidence," John said, humbly and sincerely, but pleased.

Jillian took John's arm as the escort led them to their seats.

"That was pretty high praise," Jillian said softly to John.

"Yes, I'm amazed," he said.

"You shouldn't be," she told him. "I agree with Carson. You've got this," she said, squeezing his arm, just before they entered the gargantuan theater.

The worst thing about being up for an award is the waiting. Up until that evening, it hadn't seemed that difficult to wait. With the filming of the new movie, Jillian's book signings, and an unexpected excursion to Alaska, there just wasn't time to think much about the award ceremony. But now, with cameras all around, zooming in on the faces of nominees, and the endless introductions, film clips, and speeches, time felt like it was proceeding at a snail's pace.

When it came time to watch the film clips in the Best Supporting Actor category, the lights dimmed, and John took Jillian's hand in his, holding it so tightly she thought she might lose feeling in it. She didn't dare say anything, though. This was an important moment in John's life. Even though she had a feeling they may well be back in the same theater the very next year after his new movie came out, it also could be that this would be a "once and only" occurrence. This was every actor's dream—the Academy

Awards—to have a chance to be recognized as one of the top in the profession. She held her breath as they began to announce the nominees.

When John's name was mentioned, Jillian touched his arm with her free hand and then said a little prayer. She knew that the decision had already been made, but it made her feel better. She prayed that whatever happened, John would walk away from the evening feeling happy and honored, no matter the outcome.

The actress who announced the winner was one of Jillian's all-time favorites. Jillian's heart was pounding, and she couldn't imagine what John's must have been doing at that moment.

"And the winner of the Academy Award for Best Supporting Actor is..."

Jillian would replay the next moment over and over again in her mind for years to come.

"John D. Romano..." She didn't really hear the rest of what was said, only his name, and applause and congratulations all around them. She looked over at her husband, and he looked at her. He stood up and pulled her to her feet. He took both her hands and looked at her in a way she had never seen before. He pulled her hands to his face and kissed them, his eyes still on hers, then he turned toward the aisle and rushed up to the podium, after being congratulated by Carson and others on his way.

He was congratulated by the presenters, and one of them put the golden award into his hand as he walked to the microphone.

John paused a moment, took a breath, and looked into the cameras. "I am a very thankful man tonight. I would like to thank the Academy for this great honor. I would like to thank the writers, director, and other talented actors who worked on this film. It was the perfect project with which to re-enter the world of film acting.

"And I am so thankful for the gift of working in this profession. A few years ago, something like this would have been impossible for me. I was not in a good place. But God brought a special person into my life, and since then, I've become a... new creation. I would like to nominate, and award, my wife Jillian, with the best supporting spouse award, for being the best person I've ever known, for loving and supporting me in every way, and for changing my life forever. I'll love you forever, Jillian. And I know you don't believe it, but none of this would have ever happened without you. So again, I am a very thankful man tonight. Thank you, everyone, and good night."

The music came up, and John was escorted backstage.

Jillian was so astonished by John's words that she barely noticed the cameras zooming in on her during John's speech. She wasn't certain what happened during the rest of the awards ceremony. She clapped when others clapped and watched the screen when the lights dimmed, but it was difficult to think about anything other than the fact that the man she loved so very much, had just had one of his biggest dreams come true. She felt like she had won the award right along with him, but deep inside she knew that she had won an even better award than that. She was married to John D. Romano.

Jillian thought the paparazzi had been bad before, but now they were ridiculous. The rest of the evening both she and John, either together or separately, had their photos snapped at every turn, and were asked a million questions. Jillian thought that she would hate it, but considering John had won and was so happy, it was difficult to not enjoy every minute of this special night.

They briefly attended an "after-the-awards" party, feeling it would be rude not to do so, especially with John being one of the winners. They talked with many people, and Jillian again had many people ask about her gown. She must have said Marianna's name at least two dozen times before the night was over, and sent her a text message around midnight telling her that her creation was a huge hit and to expect to be contacted by a good number of people after this night.

Hours later, John and Jillian found themselves in the back of the limousine and finally heading home. "Oscar" sat on a little table in front of them. It was so heavy that they didn't worry about it tipping over, even on the curves.

Jillian looked at John, who was gazing at the statue.

"It was such a special night, wasn't it, John?" she asked.

He turned to her. He had that same special look in his eyes as earlier. "Yes, this was a special night, but it can't hold a candle to the one eleven months minus one day ago," he said.

She smiled as she realized that he was referring to their wedding day. "Yes, agreed, that day was pretty special," she answered coyly.

"And so was the night, as I remember," he said, moving closer to her and putting his arm around her shoulders.

"Agreed on that point, as well," she said, putting her left hand and her right cheek against his chest. She fell silent as she thought about all the things he had said during his speech that night. She was so happy that they had recorded the show, so she could watch it sometime and listen to his loving words over and over again. He kissed the top of her head, and then joined her in quietude the rest of the way home.

After giving the exhausted limo driver a well-deserved tip for all his time and patience, they entered the foyer. Just to their right, through the French doors, they could see the moonlight streaming into the library through the many windows, shining down on the glass award case, as if it was anticipating its new arrival.

They walked over to the case, almost ceremoniously. Jillian opened the glass cabinet doors, and John put "Oscar" inside, then gently closed it. He looked at it for a long moment, then turned to Jillian, and took her hands.

He looked into her eyes and spoke softly. "You know, for years, I thought that my life would never be complete unless I won one of those," he said, nodding at the award. "Now, I understand that it is a fantastic recognition—a great honor—and I am very grateful. But now I also know that there are even greater honors in life— like being loved by you. Everything else pales in comparison." He let go of her hands and pulled her close, kissing her with every ounce of passion he possessed.

Finally, Jillian pulled back slowly and looked up at him. She felt the pressure of tears of happiness behind her eyes as she looked straight into his and said, "And the winner is...John D. Romano... the best husband I could have ever asked for."

Chapter Nineteen

It took several days to completely recover from "Oscar Night." Fortunately, John and Jillian had little on the agenda, although Jillian needed to prepare for her tour on the East Coast. She was not relishing packing. Her books were already on their way to their first destinations; some of them in the first leg had already been received.

Worse than the packing was the thought of being away from home, and especially John, for sixteen days. When the tour was first planned, it hadn't sounded so bad. Now, reality had set in, and it sounded like an eternity to her.

At least there were some good distractions to keep her mind occupied before she left. The first was the meeting they were going to have later in the day with Carson Stone. Jillian was intrigued by his request that she come along as well, and couldn't imagine what he had on his mind that included her.

The other was the upcoming baptism of the twins, Gus and Grace, on Sunday morning. That would take place just hours before she flew to Durham, North Carolina, where she would be appearing at a bookstore and speaking at a conference at Duke

University. She was nervous about the conference, never dreaming that her book would be so seriously considered. She had one other such conference appearance on her schedule as well, the second one in New Haven, Connecticut, at Yale University, her final stop on the tour.

She tried to shake off her trepidation as she walked into the Christian bookstore where she was picking up the Children's Bibles and books of children's prayers she had ordered for the babies. The Bibles were stamped with their names and baptism date.

She hadn't given it a thought that she might be recognized in the store, but she was indeed. "Oscar Night" most likely had something to do with that, but her book was also getting more exposure. In fact, there was a display of them just inside the door on a table.

A woman who was looking at one of them, turned to her and stared. "Is this you?" she finally asked, turning to the photo on the inside cover.

"Yes, it is," Jillian said.

The woman asked her to autograph a copy after she paid for it, and Jillian agreed. Of course, that set off a chain reaction, as others realized an author was in the store. The woman behind the counter was the store owner. She was thrilled because she was selling more books than usual, and enthusiastically pulled out a pen for Jillian to sign the copies. The owner asked if she would sign one for her, too, and Jillian was happy to accommodate.

Some people were curious to see what Jillian had ordered from the store, and some of them inquired about the stamped Bibles. The owner was ecstatic by the time Jillian bid them all farewell, an hour after walking into the store to simply pick up an order. She felt like she was getting a glimpse into John's life. He was having trouble adjusting from being pretty much a "has-been" actor who had been recognized once in a while, to a new Oscar winner whose face was now splashed across magazines, the

Internet, television, and the silver screen, and who was considered to be making one of the biggest comebacks in Hollywood at the moment.

Jillian returned home with just enough time to show John the gifts, then hop into the Land Rover with him to head to the meeting with Carson Stone.

Carson's office was ultra-modern, on the top floor of a building near the studio. John and Jillian took the elevator up, holding hands until the doors opened. They walked to the receptionist's desk and announced their arrival.

"Welcome," the pleasant woman said. "I will let Mr. Stone know you are here."

They took a seat, but not for very long. The woman called to them moments later, and then opened the door to an office just behind her.

The room was bright with daylight from all the windows on three sides. The views were breathtaking. Carson stood up from behind his glass desk and walked over to greet them. He took Jillian's hand and kissed it again. Then he shook John's hand and congratulated him on his win once more, exclaiming that the Academy occasionally gets something right.

"Just wait until next year," Carson said seriously. He was not shy about making predictions apparently. "Have a seat," he added, pointing to a luxurious couch.

John and Jillian sat down, sinking into the soft, pale gray leather.

"Let me get right to the point. A movie script came across my desk a few weeks ago. It is what I would consider to be on equal ground with our latest venture, but this time set in the medical community. I am hoping, John, that you feel like reprising a role as a surgeon. You would be fantastic as the male protagonist in the story.

"The story and concept are wonderful, but the screenwriter needs some help cleaning up the script, I believe. He has great and fresh ideas—that's why I'm taking a chance on him—but it is his first major project. He also has little medical knowledge, and I want his script to be credible. That's where you come in, Jillian. I know and trust your medical knowledge, and I just read your book, so I know you have writing skills as well. I would like you to work with him on tightening up the script, and then I am hoping that you would consider working as one of my assistants during the filming."

Jillian wasn't certain what to say at first. "I don't have any experience with screenwriting or directing, Mr. ... Carson."

"I know that, but you have genuine knowledge, and I like the way you think. You are creative, intelligent, and work well under pressure. You really helped us out in Alaska, and I would appreciate you being a part of our team on this film."

Turning to John, he continued, "I am hoping you will *both* come on board. It was a pleasure working with someone of your talent, John."

John and Jillian turned to one another, then smiled and nodded to each other.

In unison they asked, "When do we start?"

Carson spent the next half of an hour explaining his tentative timeline. The project, he hoped, would be ready to shoot by sometime that summer, depending on how quickly the script could be finished. He understood that Jillian's current commitments needed to be met first and foremost.

Carson shook John's hand, and kissed Jillian's again. She really did feel like royalty when he did that.

John and Jillian walked to the elevator in silence. The light above the doors went on, there was a "ding," and they stepped inside. The doors closed, and Jillian looked at John.

"What just happened?" she asked in an astonished voice.

"We both just got a job—and we get to work together," he said, taking her hand in his.

"I don't deserve this, John. I don't know what Carson is thinking," she said, unsure of herself.

"I do," he replied, squeezing her hand. "Don't underestimate yourself, Jillian. You have many gifts to share, and perhaps this is the beginning of an entirely new way of doing just that. You will get a chance to write in a new way. Just think of how many people's lives you can touch through the avenue of film."

"I just never considered that as an option. I guess I'm just very surprised," she said.

"Surprises can be really good things sometimes," he said, taking her chin in his hand. "I'm looking at one of the best ones in my life right now."

Just then, the elevator stopped. The door opened and gave its obligatory "ding."

"Saved by the 'ding,'" Jillian said, smiling.

John reluctantly removed his hand from her face. "Later," John said softly as they stepped out of the elevator.

John and Jillian met with Pete, Kelly, and their priest at St. Paul's Episcopal Church an hour before the worship service. The priest showed them where to stand, where to find the service for Holy Baptism in *The Book of Common Prayer,* and gave other general instructions.

The twins had been home for a month already and were growing like weeds, as Jillian's dad used to say. They were dressed in special gowns made out of the satin material from Kelly's wedding dress and sewn by Kelly's mother.

After the instructions, John and Jillian talked to Pete and Kelly's family members, many of whom they had met at the couple's wedding. They were all so thrilled about the babies and the baptisms, and so grateful that everyone was doing so well.

Kelly's mother had hugged Jillian so hard she thought she might have bruised a rib. With tears in her eyes, she had thanked Jillian for her help with getting her daughter to the hospital in time to avoid a terrible tragedy. Jillian understood the woman's sentiments, knowing what it felt like to worry about a daughter's health and survival. She cringed just thinking about Marty and her brush with a dangerous disease.

"I was just very happy that Pete called me when he did," Jillian said. "He's a good husband, and a good father."

"Yes, he is," the woman agreed, looking at her son-in-law with admiration as he held both babies in his huge, strong arms, beaming with love and pride. Jillian quickly snapped a photo of that endearing pose with her phone, then made certain it was turned off as they got ready to sit down in the pew.

The church was nearly full that morning, especially the front pews—a rarity—which brimmed with the family and friends of Pete and Kelly. The music was wonderful as it was pumped out of a huge pipe organ, superbly played by a slight man who was dwarfed by the instrument. The message, too, was very inspirational, and Jillian thought the priest did a nice job of incorporating the promises of baptism with the gospel lesson.

After the sermon, it was time to go to the large and ornate baptismal font in the front of the sanctuary. Pete and Kelly insisted that John and Jillian hold the babies. John had asked earlier if he could hold Grace Jillian, and Jillian presented August Peter for Holy Baptism.

Pete, Kelly, John, and Jillian vowed to bring up the children in the Christian faith and life, with God's help. Then with the whole congregation, they confessed their faith and prayed for Gus and Grace. They took turns holding each child over the font as they were baptized in the name of the Father, Son, and Holy Spirit, and again as they were marked with oil and the sign of the cross on their foreheads, sealed by the Holy Spirit and marked as Christ's forever. Gus slept right through it all, but Grace was wide-eyed throughout, her eyes flashing when the warm water splashed on her forehead.

Jillian looked at Pete and Kelly. Their eyes were filled with tears of joy. She instinctively turned to Pete and handed him Gus, and John gently handed Grace to Kelly, to be welcomed by the congregation. The congregation then sang a special hymn for baptism as the family and godparents were seated.

As Jillian sat down, she felt more centered than she had in a long time. There was nothing like being reminded of one's identity as a child of God to put the rest of life into perspective. She felt uplifted, strengthened, and prepared. And as it turned out—that was a good thing.

Chapter Twenty

Jillian tried to sleep on the plane to Durham, to no avail. She couldn't stop thinking about the look on John's face as she had gone through security. He had tried so very hard to be cheerful as they said goodbye at the airport. It may have been his weakest acting job ever, Jillian thought to herself. She, too, gave an equally poor performance.

She put her head back on the headrest and sighed, remembering something her mother had once told her, that it was "nice to have someone to miss." Her mother shared that on the very rare occasions when her father, Martin, would go to a convention or for new training for his work. Other than that, the couple had rarely spent a day apart from one another their entire thirty-six years of marriage.

She took a folder out of the backpack at her feet and looked over her notes for the next afternoon. She wasn't concerned about the bookstore presentation, as she was well-versed in that area, but the program at Duke was another thing. It was only a small workshop, one of many different ones going on at the same time. Perhaps, she thought, no one would show up.

Jillian was shocked when the small lecture hall began to fill up the next afternoon. She was speaking as a part of the Trent Humanities in Medicine Lecture Series, and felt fairly unqualified to be doing so. She said a prayer that she would not be wishing she hadn't accepted such an honor by the end of the day.

She had worked very hard on her presentation, and her work paid off. She was surprised by the thoughtful questions of the medical students and faculty who attended. She knew they were intelligent—that wasn't the issue. She was surprised by their keen intuition and genuine caring attitude toward the people they would be serving. And she could also tell, that her own story, which she shared openly and honestly, as well as the stories of many others in her book, resonated with many people in the room on a personal basis.

When she told her own personal story about becoming a single mom, she noticed a young woman near the back of the room, whose face turned beet red and who looked like she might run out of the room in tears at any moment. The woman seemed to pull herself together as the talk turned to other subjects, but Jillian made a mental note to try to touch base with her, if possible, at the end of the lecture.

Before Jillian knew it, she was answering questions from the audience, then people were filing out of the room. She searched the crowd for the young woman with the crimson face, but she was nowhere in sight.

Jillian had been invited to sell and sign her books in the lobby for an hour following her talk, so she was escorted to a table where the boxes of books sat, wondering if anyone would buy one. She knew that medical students rarely had money to spare. She had convinced her publisher to let her sell them at a discounted price for that reason, which she thought would help to some extent.

A line started to form, and Jillian started selling and writing away. Her hand was getting sore by the end of the hour. Thank goodness there appeared to be an end in sight. She glanced up at the last person in line. It was the young woman she had been hoping to meet.

The student timidly paid for the book, looking sad. Jillian asked her if she wanted it made out to anyone.

"Amy," she said quietly.

Jillian signed the book and handed it to her, looking her straight in the eyes.

"Amy, do you have time for a cup of coffee? I'm dying for one, and I don't know where to get one," Jillian told the young woman.

The woman looked startled by the question. She started to say that she really should be going, but then changed her mind.

"Okay, I will show you," she said.

Jillian closed up the boxes of books, covered them with a small tarp that was sitting next to the boxes, and pushed them under the table.

They walked to a building next door, where there was a small coffee kiosk with some comfortable-looking chairs nearby.

"You'll join me, won't you, Amy?" Jillian asked.

"I guess I could do that," she said, and ordered a chai latte.

Jillian led them to two chairs that were close together and more private. She started asking Amy about her studies and where she was from.

When she started talking about her hometown in Oklahoma, she looked very sad again. Jillian figured that if she wanted to tell her story, she would.

"Is it difficult to be far away from home, Amy?"

"No, I needed...I wanted to go somewhere...different."

"Yes, it is fun to experience new places, although it can be tough at times. My daughter, Marty, is in medical school. Right now she is only five hours away from me, but before that, we were many thousands of miles apart."

At the mention of Marty, the girl's face reddened again, and she looked teary-eyed.

"Are you okay, Amy?" Jillian asked softly.

"Yes...no...I don't know," she said, sniffling.

Jillian pulled a tissue out of her purse, handed it to the young woman, and waited for her to continue, if she could.

After a minute of silence, Amy spoke again. "I have...I had... a daughter once," she said. "I...I...gave her away!" Now she was crying harder. Jillian let her for a minute, then put her hand on her arm.

"So, you put her up for adoption?" Jillian asked.

"Yes, I gave my baby away. I was sixteen. I didn't really want to, but my parents said I should. I abandoned her," she said guiltily.

"Amy, let me tell you another story," Jillian said, and then proceeded to tell her story of being adopted and what it meant to her.

"Don't you hate your mother for giving you up?" Amy asked.

"Not at all, Amy. In fact, if I could, I would thank her for loving me enough to give me the home and parents that I grew up with. She knew that she could not raise a child on her own, and wanted the best life for me. She made *my* life, *my* future, her priority, and I would say that that is what a *great* mother would do for her child."

The young woman wiped her eyes and gradually stopped crying.

"I just feel so bad," she said. "I'll never see her grow up. I signed something that said I wouldn't see her. I wish I hadn't done that."

"You made a great sacrifice on behalf of your baby, Amy," Jillian said. "I know that you probably won't ever meet her—although it might happen someday when she's a legal adult—but I think in the meantime, you could try living your life to the fullest and be the best person you can be, in honor of your daughter and for any future children you may have. And be proud of the fact that you were strong enough, and loved your child enough, to give her the best possible chance in life that a young mother could possibly provide."

"I'm never going to have more children. I'll never get married," she said, starting to sniffle again. "No one is going to want to marry me."

Jillian looked at the pretty young woman and shook her head. "Never say never, Amy. If you have time, I have another story to tell you," Jillian said.

The woman nodded, and Jillian told her the story of meeting John.

"You didn't just make that up, did you?" Amy asked.

"I might write books, but I don't think I'm creative enough to make that one up, Amy," Jillian said with a smile.

Their cups of coffee and latte sat cold on the table in front of them as they stood up and hugged each other. Jillian gave Amy her business card with her contact numbers on it, in case she ever wanted to talk or correspond.

"Make your daughter proud, Amy," Jillian said.

"Kaley. Her name—when she was born—I named her Kaley," Amy said.

"Make Kaley proud, Amy," Jillian said.

"I will try...I will," she replied, more strongly. She picked up her backpack and hustled away, as she was already late for her next lecture.

Jillian watched her walk quickly out of the building, and then said a prayer for Amy, for "Kaley," and for everyone like them.

Jillian was exhausted when she got to her hotel room, but that didn't stop her from calling John as soon as she dropped her luggage on the bed. He picked up on the very first ring.

"Hi, sweetheart," he said.

Just the sound of his voice gave Jillian a shot of adrenaline. She relayed the story of the lecture, but mostly talked about Amy and her story.

"Everywhere you go, you help someone, don't you?" John asked sincerely.

"I didn't intend to, but I think I was supposed to be where I was today," she said. "I just hope Amy can truly forgive herself and realize that she did a good thing, not a bad one, and move on with her life with a more positive outlook."

"It sounds like you gave her a good chance to do that, Jillian, just like you helped me," he told her.

"And you helped me," she said, wishing she was holding him close. She laid down on the bed next to the luggage and put her head on one pillow, while pulling another one to herself, hugging it tightly. They talked about John's day, but he could hear the weariness growing in her voice.

"You had better get some sleep, Jillian," he said. "Morning is going to sneak up on you quickly when your body is still on Pacific time."

"You are right," she replied with resignation in her voice, not really wanting to hang up.

"I'll love you forever," he said sweetly.

"I'll love you forever," she answered back. She hit the end call button on her phone, set her alarm, and fell fast asleep on top of the bed, snuggling up to her carry-on.

Jillian's bookstore tour continued up the Eastern coastline. It felt like a "piece of cake" to do her usual presentation and signings after giving the lecture at Duke. She was grateful for that feeling after the draining stress of the previous day, not only from her speaking engagement but from the personal talk with Amy. She thought about the young "pre-med" student and wondered more about her family back home.

Jillian knew that she had really been fortunate that not only had she been twenty-two when Marty was born, but that she had such supportive and understanding parents. Martin and Judy Johnson had welcomed Marty into their family, and helped Jillian as much as they were able to in so many ways in her first years as a single parent. She realized more and more, the older she got, how very fortunate she was. Not everyone had a family that loved and supported their child, and grandchild, like hers had. And others may have wanted to help their children and grandchildren, but just didn't have the resources. Yes, she was truly blessed in so many ways.

Jillian thoroughly enjoyed the scenery over the next week, the mix of countryside, bustling cities, and ocean views. The tour took her through Virginia, Washington, D.C., Maryland, Delaware, New Jersey, New York, and to her final designation at Yale. She would be giving a talk similar to the one she had given at Duke. Both universities had excellent schools not only in medicine but in theology, and valued the connection between the physical and the spiritual aspects of human life.

The evening before her lecture, Jillian looked over the conference schedule for her appearance at Yale. She felt more comfortable about the situation, having had such a favorable response at Duke. She thought she might even be able to relax that night. That is, until she turned to page ten of the conference presenters' pamphlet.

There he was. She stared at the photo of a face that appeared to be looking right at her. It had been almost twenty-seven years since she had seen that face—the face of Dr. Jeffrey A. Lawrence, the biological father of her daughter. Jillian caught her breath.

After the initial shock wore off, Jillian read through his bio. He was still teaching at the medical school she had briefly attended, but was now chair of his department. A long list of accomplishments and publications were listed, along with mention of an award he had recently received. Even in his fifties, he was still very attractive, with a cleft in his chin and dimples in his cheeks. His thick, blonde hair looked like it was just beginning to gray at the temples, but instead of detracting from his looks, it made him look commanding and distinguished.

Dr. Lawrence was presenting two hours before Jillian in a huge lecture hall in the same building in which she would be lecturing. After her speaking engagement, she would be signing books just outside her presentation room.

Her heart was pounding, and suddenly she understood how John must have felt when he found out his co-star in the pipeline movie would be Monica Morgan. He had almost turned down the job because of it. Jillian wished she could turn down her lecture the next day, but it was too late for that. She sat down in the armchair in the hotel room in a fog.

Jillian had spoken to John just a few hours before. He had called her and in an ecstatic voice relayed the news that he had gotten a last-minute call from the *Tonight Show*. He would be leaving for New York City at six the next morning from LAX. He would be picked up by a limo, taken to the studio to be prepped for the show, go to makeup, and go on the air. He was very excited, and rightly so. His only regret was that she could not be there. He told her he would call her as soon as the they were done filming and that maybe he would be able to see her, even if just for an hour or so.

She almost picked up the phone, but if she did that, John would probably be up all night. She decided that she would just have to tough this one out alone. Perhaps she would get an opportunity to talk to John in the morning, but then again, she didn't want to upset him before his appearance on the show. He had waited years for this kind of success and recognition in his field, and calling him with unsettling news would not be considerate in the least.

Jillian laid awake for hours that night, hypnotized by a blinking green light on some sort of monitor on the ceiling. She did a lot of thinking, and even more praying. A year-and-a-half before, Jillian had laid awake wondering why God would allow her to end up at the home of John D. Romano. The answer had played out in a most amazing way, much better than she could have ever imagined. She couldn't imagine at the moment, however, what kind of good could come out of this situation, but prayed that somehow it would.

Jillian wondered if their paths would cross, and if they did, if Jeffrey would even recognize her or remember what had transpired between them. Jillian panicked for a moment that if he did remember, it might affect all of their lives and somehow thwart John's plans to adopt Marty.

Jillian couldn't understand why, when her life was so happy and settled, this ripple—no, this wave—would come crashing into her world. She decided she would just have to wait and see, and would have to turn this one over to God.

The next afternoon, Jillian set up her book-signing display in the hallway, covered it with the tarp, then entered the small lecture room. There was no one presenting before her, so she put her materials on the podium in front. She set up her computer. A screen was already down and ready for her visuals.

Kathy J. Jacobson

Jillian sat down in one of the seats in the front row and took a deep breath, when a strange feeling came over her. Suddenly she found herself compelled toward the door and down the hallway to the other section of the building. She stopped just outside the wide, opened doors and glanced into the large assembly hall, which was nearly full. She found herself attached to a small contingent of people entering the room at the last minute, taking a seat in one of the last rows off to one side, ready to listen to the famed Dr. Jeffrey A. Lawrence expound on his latest work.

Over an hour later, Jillian watched Dr. Lawrence basking in the attention he was getting as many people stayed to speak with him. There was no doubt in her mind that he was still brilliant. There was no doubt in her mind that he was still good-looking. And there was no doubt in her mind that he was highly aware of both of those facts.

Jillian slid out of her seat and walked out of the lecture hall. She returned to her room in perfect time to meet with the tech person and give her a few directions. For whatever reason, Jillian felt remarkably calm. Quite frankly, giving a presentation felt normal and seemed almost relaxing after the unusual experience of the past hour.

A good-sized audience assembled in the room for Jillian's talk. It was a very inquisitive and respectful group of people, who seemed genuinely interested in the subject of her book, much like the group at Duke had been. They asked intelligent questions and were an engaging group.

When their time was up and they had dispersed from the room, Jillian put her computer and papers in her case to get ready to go to the book-signing table. She smiled to herself as she walked to the door, thinking that she had indeed made the right decision to do this tour and the presentations. That feeling made an exit a short time later.

A number of people were in line to buy a book and have it signed. She began selling and signing, briefly speaking to the students and a few professors as she did. Out of the corner of Jillian's eye, she noticed a fairly noisy group of people coming down the hallway, surrounding someone. It reminded her of the paparazzi swarming around the Oscar winners. She wondered who the "star" was in this case.

She glanced back after signing a book and saw who was attracting so much attention. In the middle of his "fans" was Dr. Jeffrey A. Lawrence, looking important and pleased as the entourage seemed to hang on his every word. They stopped near the end of line for the book signing, and Jeffrey bid them goodbye. He stood alone for a moment, appearing to wait for someone. One of the young women turned around, came back, and spoke to him.

Jillian watched his face. She had seen that look before. At the end of their conversation, Jillian watched him take what looked like a hotel key card and hand it to the young woman. She said something to him, and he said something back, very quietly.

The next moment, he looked annoyed as he pulled a cell phone out of his pocket. He nodded to the young woman, smiling that dimpled smile of his, and then she was off. The smile faded from his face, and he scowled as he spoke into the phone, and then to Jillian's shock, he got into the line for her book.

It took everything she had to concentrate on each person as they spoke to her and she signed their books, some with special greetings. She sincerely hoped that she was not so distracted that she made any mistakes in any of them. She sent up a little prayer for strength and help.

Jeffrey was getting closer to the front of the line. Jillian signed a book for a woman who must have been one of his colleagues. The woman spoke to Jeffrey as she turned from the table and noticed him in the line.

"Jeffrey," she said in a sweet voice. "I didn't take you as the type for this book." Her voice had a slightly teasing tone.

"My wife insisted I get a copy for her," he grumbled.

Then he was at the front of the line, standing right in front of Jillian. He pulled some cash out of his wallet and handed it to her. She made change with sweaty palms. Jillian could tell that blood was rushing to her face. It felt like it was on fire, and her heart was leaping against her rib cage. He didn't seem to recognize her—in fact, he barely looked at her until she asked him how she should sign the book.

"Make it out to Rachel," he said in an exasperated tone.

Jillian's hands were shaking, and it took a moment to steady the pen in her right hand. She could feel his eyes on her as she signed the book. She looked up, and he was staring at her. She thought for a moment that he was remembering her, and when he smiled that dimpled smile, she felt like running away.

"Are you staying here for the entire conference?" he asked, suddenly in a nicer tone. "I'm busy tonight, but I'm free tomorrow night if you'd like to catch a drink...to talk about your book, of course." He added this last part unconvincingly, and Jillian was pretty sure that he said it just in case there was someone he knew listening to the conversation.

"I leave this evening. In fact, I hope to meet my husband in the city," she said.

"Pity," he replied, and took the book from her.

"I hope your wife enjoys the book," Jillian said, feeling so very sorry for Rachel, the unfortunate woman who was married to Dr. Jeffrey A. Lawrence.

He gave a small grunt and was gone.

There were only a few more customers after that. Jillian packed up her display and covered it again. It would be picked up later by the same person who had dropped off the boxes.

She looked at her watch. It was five p.m. Any moment now, John would be sitting next to the host of the talk show, chatting about his Academy Award and the new movie due out in a few months. She wished she could have changed her presentation time so she could have been there for him. Because of her commitments, she wasn't even able to call and tell him to "break a leg." Instead, she said a prayer for him that all was going well. It was the best that she could do, and after she thought about it some more, it *was* the best thing that she could have done for him.

She finished her silent litany, and her cell phone buzzed. It was her agent, calling to check in to see how things had gone and to give her some exciting news. Her book had just made the *New York Times* best-seller list for non-fiction. Jillian almost dropped the phone.

John sat next to the talk show host, who took a sip of coffee and went to a commercial break. They had just finished discussing John's role as Mack and his Academy Award. John had been nervous at first, but the audience was so warm and receptive that he was now feeling quite at ease.

They came back from the break and talked about the premise of the new movie, then played a film clip. The audience clapped, and they returned to their talk.

"What was it like to be reunited on screen with Monica Morgan?" the host asked.

"It was a unique experience," John answered tactfully. "We have known each other for a very long time, and certainly our prior work together gave us an advantage in many ways." Then he added with sincerity, "Monica is also a very talented actor. She always had natural ability, but having the space of many years between our projects, it gave me a chance to see how she has really developed as an artist over the years."

"And I am certain that she would say the same of you, as your recent achievements have proven," the host said. "You've had quite a comeback, and many are saying that you are better than ever. What has caused this big turnaround, would you say?"

"It's not a what," John said, "it's a 'who.'"

"I would assume you are speaking about your wife? That was quite the speech you gave at the Oscars. You are obviously a very happily married man."

"That would be an understatement," John replied. "In every respect, the past eleven months, two weeks, and five days have been the best days of my life."

"Not that's he's counting, folks," the host quipped, smiling. "And I understand that your wife...," he paused and looked at his paper.

"Jillian Johnson Romano," John filled in the blank for him.

"Yes, she is an author, correct?"

"Yes, she recently published a non-fiction book, *Where Broken Hearts Go*, that is doing very well. In fact, she would be here if she was able, but she is speaking at a medical conference at Yale. Her work is being taken very seriously, especially since she worked in the nursing profession for many years," John said proudly.

The host pulled out a copy of Jillian's book from behind the desk, and the camera zoomed in on it. He continued on, "And it has come to our attention this afternoon that the book has now reached the *New York Times* best-seller list, John."

John face lit up in happy surprise. He looked straight into the camera. "Way to go, Jillian. You deserve it, sweetheart," he said unashamedly.

"So you fully endorse her work, I would imagine," the host said.

"I know for a fact that she knows what she's talking about, because she took my heart and put it back together," he replied seriously.

"You heard it here, folks," the host said. "John, it was wonderful having you on the show. Congratulations on your award, congratulations on your new movie, and congratulations on your marriage. How are you going to celebrate your first anniversary?"

"We are going to cut the ribbon on our non-profit acting workshop, 'The Esperanza Workshop,' in Los Angeles. We feel very blessed, and hope to share some of those blessings with others who haven't had the advantages that we have had."

"That sounds great, John. I look forward to hearing more about that in the future," the host said. He then turned to the camera and mentioned who his guests would be on the next episode, then they cut.

The host shook John's hand. "I really do want to hear more about your project, John," he said. "It if does well, will you open one here in New York?"

"We are thinking big, so I won't say that hasn't crossed our minds. We would love to see them all across the country one day, but for now we will focus on the first one and see how it goes. Of course, if you or anyone else wants to learn more about how to get one going, or something like it, please give me a call." John took out his private business card and gave it to the host.

Then John shook hands with him again, and also shook hands with some of the crew and even a few of the fans who were waiting around at the bottom of the stage, which endeared him to them for life.

Just as John got back to the green room to pick up his coat and small travel case, his phone, which was on silent, flashed a text from Jillian. He picked it up and checked the message.

Call me when u r done.

John called her immediately, and she answered on the second ring.

"What took you so long?" John asked teasingly.

"Just a little tired, I guess," she said, trying not to sound as completely and emotionally whipped as she felt at that moment, to little avail. John was much too in tune with her to miss the inflection in her voice.

"What's going on, sweetheart?" he asked.

"It's over now, but I have a lot to tell you," she said. "It's not really phone conversation material, unfortunately."

"Well, then it's really a good thing that Alan got my flight changed to tomorrow morning, the same as yours. My driver is going to bring me out to you in just a bit, unless you have a commitment this evening?" he asked, knowing that she may very well have something. "I'll wait for you if you need to meet with someone."

"There's only one person I need to meet with, and I'm speaking to him right now. Oh, John, this is the best surprise!" She wanted to say that it was much better than the other surprise she had just been dealt, but didn't want to go into it on the phone. "I can't wait to see you, John," she said softly, her eyes misty.

"Same here," John said. He checked with Jillian to make certain he had the correct address for her hotel, and told her he hoped to see her in an hour. "Should we have some dinner when I get there, or will you have already eaten?" he asked.

"How about room service?" Jillian suggested. If they went out, it would take up the entire evening. They would also have to deal with all the people recognizing John. Plus, she also had a lot of very personal things to tell him, which would be better said in a private setting. And most of all, she selfishly wanted him all to herself.

"Sounds perfect," he said. "I love you, Jillian."

"I love you, too, John. I can't wait to see you."

They hung up. John was shown out the back door, where the limo driver was waiting. There were a few fans waiting for him too. He shook hands and signed some autographs, and then they were off to Connecticut.

Jillian was doing well until she opened the door and looked into John's eyes. She was so overwhelmed by seeing him, especially after the events of the day, that she practically jerked him inside of the room. She held on to him like she was holding on for dear life, and tears flooded her eyes.

"Jillian, what's wrong?" John asked, pulling back and looking at her with concern in his eyes.

"Actually, I think the question is 'what's right,' and the answer would be 'you.' I am so incredibly grateful to be married to *you*, John D. Romano."

"What brought this on?" he inquired gently, smiling and stroking her hair, but still sensing that there was more to the story.

"I'll tell you in a bit. First things, first," she said, and kissed him deeply.

"That was worth the entire trip east," he said after their lips parted.

There was a knock on the door, and a voice called, "Room service."

Jillian knew John's favorites on the menu and had ordered several selections. A tall and handsome young man, whose name tag said he was "Henry," rolled in a cart and set up dinner on a small round table in the room, complete with a candle and a flower in a vase. John tipped him generously, and he was out the door with a big smile on his face.

John opened a bottle of wine and gave a toast to Jillian on making the best-seller list. She was surprised that he knew about it as she hadn't yet told him. Then she made a toast to him in honor of his appearance on the *Tonight Show*.

Jillian didn't share her story immediately, deciding that it was better told on a full stomach. She was ravenous, and suddenly realized that she had skipped lunch in all the "excitement" of the day. As they finished eating, John looked at her expectantly. Jillian was beginning to feel better already, and she hadn't even relayed the story. Just being with John was balm, and eating some food helped her get back on a more even keel.

"Okay, Jillian, as our daughter would most likely put it, 'spill.'"

She smiled a weak smile and began the story of the past twenty-four hours. John listened attentively to every word, trying not to comment or react until she was done. Toward the end of the saga, when she relayed how Jeffrey had propositioned her, she could see John's hand clenching into a fist. She had only seen that happen one other time, when little Rick was being gruffly and rudely spoken to by his father during a Christmas meal that they had shared together over a year ago.

"I always wondered what would happen if this day ever really came. In my mind, I thought that perhaps the biological father of my child would have turned over a new leaf, become a new creation over time. I felt sorry for him, and in a way for Marty, that he seemed no better than he was many years ago, and in some ways, even worse. And I felt disappointed in myself, for having been attracted to, and having 'given in,' to someone like him. It's hard to believe that he and Marty are actually related. The only things she inherited from him are her brilliant mind for medicine, her dimples, and her thick, blonde hair—thank goodness." She reached for John's hand across the table. "In every other way, she takes after her *real* father," she said.

"And don't forget her mother," John replied, rubbing her hand with his fingers. "Jillian, you are the main reason Marty is the special woman she is today."

Jillian squeezed his hand. "As I said before, I am so grateful to be married to *you*, John D. Romano," she said, the candlelight shining in her eyes, which were getting dewy again.

"And I, you, Jillian Johnson Romano," he said, penetrating her inmost being with the love in his eyes.

Jillian propped up the pillows on the bed shortly before the *Tonight Show* aired, making sure that they were both settled before the start. John had set the DVR at the last moment before he left the house, but Jillian wanted to see it like millions of others were seeing it. She was still very disappointed about not being there for the taping, but having the unexpected pleasure of being able to watch it in John's warm, strong arms was erasing those regrets by the second.

She was mesmerized by the interview, feeling such pride as she watched him so ably answer the host's questions. They came to the segment where they talked about her book and showed a close-up of it. Jillian was astonished, now knowing how John knew about the best-seller list. Her cell phone went off a moment later. She didn't answer it right away, as she listened to John's sweet response to the news, talking straight into the camera to her.

She did *not* want to answer the phone at that moment, but she saw that it was her agent, so she reluctantly picked it up, wanting to kiss John so badly as the commercial break began.

"Did you just see that?" asked her agent, who was in New York on business.

"I certainly did," Jillian responded happily, with John rubbing her back as she sat up in the bed.

"Get ready, Jillian. If you thought the book was doing well before, just wait," her agent said excitedly.

"Thank you, I will," she said. "Oh, sorry, please excuse me, I've got to go. I have something I have to do."

They said goodbye, and John looked at her inquisitively.

"Did you forget something you had to do?" he asked as the next commercial came on.

"Yes...this," she said, leaning down toward him and kissing him.

The show came back on, and Jillian sat back up. "Saved by the show," she said to him, using some of his usual words to her in similar situations.

After the host signed off, Jillian turned to John. "That was wonderful, John. Not only did you nail the interview, even the Esperanza Workshop got exposure. That certainly cannot hurt our plans for the future," she said, smiling.

John went on to tell her that the host had seemed genuinely interested in the project and wondered about the possibility of a future workshop in New York City.

"All of our hopes, our dreams—they're starting to come true, John" she said, her fingers caressing his face.

He put his hand to hers, pulled it to his lips, and kissed it gently. "No, Jillian, they already have," he said, and pulled her to himself.

Chapter Twenty-One

It took a good part of the next day to return home, but it wasn't as bad as Jillian had anticipated. She thought she would be alone on the trek west, but instead, she got to spend time with her husband, catching up on the goings-on of the past two weeks as they flew across the nation.

John mentioned how helpful Drew had been in finalizing all the accounting aspects, and Robert and his associate on the remaining legal odds and ends for the Esperanza Workshop. Brooks and Bobbi had announced that not only were they ready to begin auditions for students at the workshop the day after the ribbon cutting, but they were getting married in June in Minnesota. They felt that the Esperanza Workshop project was a real gift to them, as they could use their acting and directing skills, but also lead a normal lifestyle. They were hoping to start a family in the not-too-distant future, and that would be much more possible now that they would have a steady income and reasonable work schedules.

John also informed Jillian that Carson had sent over a preliminary synopsis and script for both of them to look over when they got a chance.

"Never a dull moment, is there?" John asked, as he took her hand.

"No, not really, but I don't mind too much when the things are good things. It will be nice to have a few days off, though, for our anniversary," she said, smiling at the thought.

Both she and John had told their agents they were not working or auditioning the weekend of their first anniversary, and their requests had been honored.

"What do you want to do for our anniversary, Jillian?"

"Maybe dinner with our family or friends? It doesn't really matter to me, as long as whatever we do, we do it together," she said, meaning it.

"Agreed," he said, his hand tightening around hers.

Then Jillian put her head on his shoulder, and fell sound asleep until they landed.

During the two weeks preceding their anniversary weekend, Jillian was interviewed for the book review section of the *Los Angeles Times*. Making the *New York Times* best-seller list and the *Tonight Show* exposure had really rocketed interest in her book, and her agent added the interview and a few extra book signings to her already busy agenda. When she wasn't talking about her book, she was writing her regular blog posts and working on her new book.

She was exhausted, but ecstatic, when it was finally time for her and John's special celebratory four-day weekend, which began on Friday and would end with the ribbon cutting at the Esperanza Workshop on Monday. Jillian hardly remembered what it felt like to sleep in and have nowhere that either of them had to be. On Saturday night, they would celebrate their anniversary with Marty and Michael, who were coming down to their house for dinner. John told Jillian that he was taking care of everything for the meal. She wasn't quite sure what that meant—if he was cooking or having something ordered in. Either sounded great to her. All she cared about was celebrating the most special event of her life, with the most special people in her life.

Their actual anniversary was on Monday, thus the ribbon-cutting ceremony on that day of the week. They couldn't think of a better anniversary gift than opening the center, and had agreed that would be their gift to one another. It was one of the few occasions they actually cued the press as to a happening in their lives. They hoped the publicity would generate donations to help keep the workshop operational and eventually expand their work. Their dream was to add health care, reading classes, and other arts to their repertoire in the future, if all went well.

After sleeping in a second day in a row, but still rising early by many people's standards, John made Jillian breakfast, then asked if she wanted to go hiking. Jillian thought that was a fantastic idea, as it had been too long since she had been outside for any period of time. She exercised at hotels every day on her tour, but it wasn't the same as being out in nature and fresh air. John, too, had mainly used the gym at home lately, and was anxious to be out and about.

They filled a backpack with sandwiches, fruit, trail mix, and plenty of water, grabbed their hiking boots and socks, and headed out to Eaton Canyon near Pasadena. It was on their list of places they wanted to hike, but had not made it to yet. The park included a four-mile trail, a forty-foot waterfall, and a nature center.

Because it was early in the hiking season for many Californians, it was not too busy when they arrived. John and Jillian both put on sunglasses and baseball caps, laced up their boots, and were off. It must have been too early in the morning for the paparazzi, as no one had followed them out of town, thankfully.

It was a perfect weather day, much like the same Saturday had been the year before. The hike was invigorating, and the fresh air made them hungry, even after a larger-than-normal breakfast. Near the end of their hike, they found a quiet spot on a rock to sit, checking for rattlesnakes before they settled down on top of it. Jillian thought it was funny how peanut butter and honey on whole grain bread tasted like a delicacy after a hike outside. There was something about eating on the trail that made everything taste better than usual. She and John clinked their metal water bottles together in a toast, then enjoyed their simple meal.

After eating, they continued on to the waterfall. There was something about waterfalls that always put Jillian into a bit of a trance. She stared at it, just listening to the rushing water and enjoying the sun shining on her skin, and thinking about the past year.

"A penny for your thoughts," John said, turning to her and putting his arms gently around her.

"I feel like the blessings I've had in the past year being married to you are like the drops of water in that waterfall—countless. And together, each one of them has made something very beautiful and powerful," she said.

He nodded his head in agreement, then cupped her chin in his fingers. "Thank you, Jillian, for the best year of my life," John said in all sincerity, then kissed her gently. Rarely did John kiss her in public, but today he just didn't care.

Jillian held him tightly and said a prayer of thanks—for their waterfall of love.

They got home an hour before Marty and Michael were due to arrive. Jillian couldn't put her finger on it, but she felt that something was "up" as they drove into the garage. It was just a feeling, but Jillian often found her feelings to be on the mark, and this time was no exception.

The kitchen seemed quiet enough, but as they headed down the hallway toward the foyer and staircase, Jillian thought she heard something. She always could hear even the tiniest hint of noise. She listened again, and just as she was going to say something to John, the lights went on, and people flooded into the foyer and hallway from the living room and library shouting, "Surprise!"

There was Marty and Michael, Jerry and Carol, Robert, Karen, and Rick, Pete and Kelly, Drew and Greta, Pastor Jim and Janet, Nancy and Buck, Alan and Beverly, and then came the kicker. Last, but not the least, a deep voice came from the living room.

"Happy Anniversary, Jillian," and out stepped Tommy, followed by Maria, John Anthony, and Alison.

Now Jillian was weeping. It took a lot to make her do that, and this was "*a lot*" in her book.

"You said you wanted to spend your anniversary with family and friends, so I invited a few," John said, grinning from ear to ear, hugging her to his side.

They spent the next ten minutes hugging, kissing, and greeting their family and friends, who had all arrived, she discovered, via a bus that had picked each of them up. Marty and Michael had been picked up at the city bus station, the Romano family at the airport, and the others at their homes. Later, the driver would take the friends back to their homes, and family would stay at the house.

The doorbell rang. John opened it, and in strode Leo with a contingent of helpers, including one of his daughters, who was a beautiful girl of eighteen named Addie. Her given name was Adelina, but she preferred her nickname at this point in her life. Jillian saw John Anthony's eyes light up and follow the young woman as she walked by carrying a huge container of tiramisu. The others, who were not members of the family, carried in huge roasters, with Leo barking at them in Italian just as he did in the kitchen in the restaurant. They went back for a second load, and John Anthony offered to help as Addie walked by.

They quickly set up, then Leo gave instructions again, and most of them got ready to go, all except Addie and one other young man who would help serve the dinner. Jillian wanted Leo to stay, but he just couldn't do that on the busiest night of the week at the restaurant. She told him she wanted to have him and his wife over some Monday evening when they were off, and that she would make something for them for a change. Leo looked pleased by the offer, and gave her one of his famous bear hugs.

"You found yourself the right one, Giovanni," Leo said to John, hugging him next.

"I certainly did," John responded.

Jillian wondered where everyone would sit. Even the large table in the dining room was not big enough for almost two dozen people. But John had thought of everything. Out on the deck there were two large tables of twelve set up, with several large outdoor heaters in case they needed them later. The small string ensemble they had had at their wedding reception was stationed nearby, ready to begin playing as they sat down.

The late afternoon was filled with chatter, and the evening with toasts and Leo's wonderful food, which they decided to serve buffet-style out of the kitchen. Afterwards, people began to dance. John had hired someone to string lights in the backyard while they had been hiking, and they twinkled on the surface of the pool.

The food from Leo's was its usual fabulous self. It didn't get much better than pasta, pizza, and parmigiana. Maria thought that perhaps she could meet with Leo sometime to share some cooking secrets. She was again impressed by his tasty fare and pronounced the pizza the best she had ever had anywhere— including her own creations.

Maria's own business was growing by leaps and bounds. She had recently hired several new employees, one of whom was very talented and trustworthy. Maria had been so relieved after that hire, especially with this weekend away planned. She really shouldn't have taken time off, but she wasn't going to miss this for anything. She had already worked the major holidays, so she felt she was entitled to a break. Tommy seemed truly relieved that she had been able to come along. He was proud of her business and very supportive, but was a bit wary of the long hours she was spending working and away from family, even with the new help.

After a few hours, Robert, Karen, and Rick were picked up by the bus. Rick had loved the pizza, and especially liked meeting Pete and John Anthony. Jillian thought it was wonderful that Rick was being introduced to so many positive male role models, especially those who were big and strong. He could see firsthand that these men didn't use their strength to overpower or abuse others, but were gentle and respectful men. It could only reinforce all the good things that he was learning in Karen and Robert's household.

The adoption process was usually a very slow and tedious one, but the soon-to-be family excitedly announced that it was looking like a summer court date might just happen after all, as Robert was pulling some strings with his legal contacts. After that announcement, John told everyone about his plans to adopt Marty. Tommy's family already knew, but it was special and exciting news to the rest of their friends. There were hugs and cheers all around.

At midnight, the last of the party attendees left on the bus. John Anthony, Alison, Marty, and Michael went to watch a movie in the theater room. Maria and Tommy asked if they could stay outside for a while, if John and Jillian didn't mind.

Jillian didn't mind—in fact, she thought that the two of them should spend some rare time alone together—and feigned that all the hiking and dancing had worn her out. In reality, she wasn't

Kathy J. Jacobson

very tired, as she felt energized by all the fun happenings of the day.

John took Jillian's hand as they walked up the stairs to their room. They left the light on in the hall for all of their guests, realizing that it was the first time that every one of their bedrooms would be full. It made them both smile when John mentioned that.

John pulled the door to the room closed behind him and walked over to Jillian, who was hanging her sweater on the back of a chair. She turned to face him as he approached.

"I hope you're not too tired..."

He didn't get the rest of his sentence out, as Jillian threw her arms around his neck and kissed him with all of her being.

"I guess you're not," he whispered.

The next day, the family went to church together. They noticed that Pastor Jim looked a bit fatigued. He rarely stayed out past ten on a Saturday night, but he and Janet had been having so much fun that they had made an exception. They thanked John and Jillian again for the wonderful evening out, and Jillian wondered what they could do to give him and Janet more breaks. Between the twins and the parish, there was little time for rest and relaxation.

After the service, they enjoyed brunch at one of their favorite restaurants, having reserved a private table in a small room in the back. John and Jillian had told the family about their hike the day before, and everyone thought that they should go on another one after they got done eating. They decided on the Solstice Canyon/ Rising Sun trail in Malibu, where the Midwesterners could take in the breathtaking views of the Pacific Ocean.

Jillian was so happy that their family members would be present for the ribbon-cutting ceremony the next morning. Michael, unfortunately, had to head north after the hike, as he had a report to give on his research, but Marty would be staying until after the ceremony, when she would catch a bus back to Stanford. Michael was getting a ride back with Jerry that evening after they dropped Carol off at the airport. Carol was not looking forward to getting on that plane, but it helped knowing that soon she would be in Los Angeles permanently. She and Jerry were so grateful that John and Jillian were buying Jerry's house, and they were going to sign the papers on the deal in a week, when Carol was back during her spring break.

John and Jillian felt honored that so many people had gone out of their ways to be present on this special weekend, squeezing in time for them in the midst of very busy schedules and commitments. People outside of their inner circle probably thought John and Jillian should have done something extravagant for their first anniversary, but this was exactly the way they wanted to celebrate it, surrounded by the love of family and friends. For John and Jillian, time spent in this manner was more than extravagant—it was *priceless*, and was something that could not be bought or replaced by anything else. It would truly be a weekend that they would not soon forget and would cherish forever.

Chapter Twenty-Two

At eleven a.m. on March the 27th, officially their first anniversary, John and Jillian stood with a huge scissors in their hands, surrounded by Marty, Tommy, Maria, John Anthony, Alison, Robert, Drew, Greta, Pete, and Esperanza. Several news stations' cameras surrounded them, along with newspaper and magazine reporters, and some of the usual paparazzi took photos as they cut through the thick blue ribbon and told the story behind the Esperanza Workshop. John gave a short speech, talking about how his life had been changed while on his wedding trip to Tanzania the summer before. He said that he had also been inspired by the example of some special people, like his and Jillian's friend, Esperanza, who both worked full-time and was a full-time college student striving to build a brighter future for herself.

"Esperanza has a great name," John said. "It means hope, and my wife, Jillian, and I want to give others hope by opening this workshop. It is just a small step, but with the help of generous people, we trust it will continue to grow and positively affect many lives in the future, here in Los Angeles and hopefully one day elsewhere."

The television stations aired that part of the speech, one of them live-streaming it as it was given, and put the link for donations across their screen and on their stations' websites. It was such an exciting morning. They took questions about the workshop for half an hour following the ceremony, then had to move off the sidewalk. The crowd of people, TV vans, and other vehicles were clogging up traffic in an already heavily trafficked area—which in L.A., was pretty much everywhere.

After talking with the press, Jillian and John climbed into the Land Rover. Some police officers helped them safely get away from the photographers and pull away from the curb. They dropped Marty off at the bus station, and then drove Tommy and his family to the airport. It was hardest of all to say goodbye to them, as they were now the ones who were the farthest away and they saw the least.

"I think we need a taste of the Midwest before we begin our next work project, don't you, John?" Jillian asked as they unloaded the family's luggage from the back of the Land Rover.

"Yes, if you can get away, I will make it work, even if it's just for a few days. We can't let it be this long between visits again. It's not good for any of us," John said seriously.

Tommy nodded his head in agreement and hugged John with tears in his eyes.

Seeing Tommy like that made Jillian feel weepy, but she tried to hold it together. She had loved Tommy from the moment she met him, maybe even before that, when she had heard the love and concern he had for John on the telephone answering machine. While too close to her age to be like a son, he sometimes felt like the younger brother Jillian had always wished she had had.

She hugged Tommy and kissed him, then did the same to Maria, John Anthony, and Alison in turn. Alison whispered to her as she hugged her that she wanted to talk to Jillian about

Kathy J. Jacobson

nursing schools the next time they got together. Jillian let go of her and looked at the young woman before her, who seemed to have grown up before her very eyes.

"I would love to do that," Jillian whispered back to her, and hugged her again.

Nobody was in the mood for a long, drawn-out goodbye, so the family headed through the automatic doors of the airport, and John and Jillian hopped back into the Land Rover, getting out of the way of an impatient driver in a Porsche who wanted their spot.

Neither of them spoke on the way home. They didn't have to, as each knew how the other was feeling, and that was enough. After the traffic thinned out a bit, John reached over and held Jillian's hand, communicating with her through his touch. She squeezed his hand gently, as if to answer him.

John and Jillian climbed into bed almost twelve hours after the ribbon-cutting ceremony, just in time to catch the eleven o'clock news and their brief segment on it. They had received texts that Marty had made it back safely to Stanford, that Michael's presentation had gone very well, and lastly that Tommy and his family had landed in Chicago.

John propped himself up on some pillows, and Jillian put her head on his chest as they watched their news piece air. When it was over, John decided that he should check his computer to see if they had received any donations yet, so he jumped out of the bed and practically ran over to his laptop, which was recharging on the dresser.

He looked, then looked again.

"Jillian, look at this," he said, unhooking and bringing the laptop over to her with an astonished look on his face.

"So, we got a few?" she asked as he walked toward her.

"I guess you could say that," he said.

Jillian gazed at the page and did a double-take, just as John had. They had already received over a hundred thousand dollars in donations, and this was only the first day. The newspaper and magazine articles hadn't even come out yet, and their online ads were not yet operational. As they stared at the numbers and names on the side of the page, the information kept refreshing itself, most likely because of the newscast minutes ago. There were donations in amounts anywhere from ten dollars to hundreds to thousands, but then suddenly, the number took an incredible jump. Both John and Jillian thought that perhaps what they were seeing was a mistake.

They hit the donor information key, and it showed an anonymous donation was made just seconds before. It was for *one million dollars*. They sat dumbfounded, wondering who they might know who had that kind of money, and who might want to give it to their project. Finally, they gave up trying to figure it out and just thanked God for whoever it was, and for their incredible generosity.

John gently closed the laptop and put it on the nightstand. He picked up the remote control and clicked off the television. He turned to Jillian, with such happiness and love in his eyes.

"Happy anniversary, sweetheart," he said.

"Yes, it's a *very* happy anniversary," she said in awe of both the donations, and even more that she had been married to this man for an entire year.

She looked at him lovingly and said, "I didn't think it was possible."

"The workshop or the donations?"

"Well, those, too. But what I really didn't think was possible was that I could love you any more than I did the day I married you, but I was wrong. Every day I wake up and start loving you even more than I did the day before," she said, stroking his face.

"Everything starts new?" he asked smiling.

"Yes, new creation, each and every day," she said smiling back at him.

He reached over and turned off the light, and moonlight streamed into the room. He moved close to Jillian and looked into her eyes.

"I'll love you forever, Mrs. Romano," John said, leaning over her, just inches from her face.

"I'll love you forever, Mr. Romano," she said, and pulled his lips to hers.

The End

Questions for Discussion

1. John and Jillian make some major changes upon returning from their wedding trip. Have you ever been inspired/influenced in the same fashion by something you experienced?

2. Pete and Kelly have a very frightening experience as new parents. Have you, or someone you know, been challenged in this way? Discuss.

3. Karen and Robert become foster parents. They had once hoped to have a family, to no avail. What kinds of risks do they face by taking in Rick? It is mentioned that perhaps Robert may have become a "workaholic" because he and Karen were unable to become parents. What are your thoughts on this? What are other ways people handle this kind of disappointment?

4. John is very excited at finding the "perfect" script until he finds out his co-star is Monica Morgan. He even considers backing out of the movie, even though it is just the project for which he has been waiting. Do you think he should have done the movie? Do you think you could have been as supportive as Jillian was in this situation?

5. Karen and Robert are going to have many new experiences as first-time parents. Jillian makes a mental note that her friends will have to adjust to how "messy life can be as parents, in so many different ways." Discuss that thought.

6. Greta seems to influence Drew in many positive ways. Have you been in a relationship with someone who made you a better person? Have you been in a relationship where you think you made someone else better?

Kathy J. Jacobson

7. Jillian makes the discovery that her new work as a writer has a similarity to her former work as a nurse—both help people heal. Do you see a similar pattern in your own endeavors?

8. Rick grew up in an unhappy, unhealthy home situation. He experiences mixed emotions when his father dies. How might you feel if you were mistreated by someone close to you, and then they died?

9. John's work includes situations which could cause even the best of relationships to suffer or end (i.e., working with members of the opposite sex—including imitate scenes with them—the paparazzi, fans, lack of privacy in daily life, long workdays, and time away from family.) Which one(s) would be the most challenging for you? Would you enjoy being married to a celebrity?

10. Some special Christmas gifts are given—the family crèche to John from Jillian and Tommy; the wood carving from Marty to John; the "key to my heart" ring from John to Jillian. Which one is your favorite, and why? Have you ever received a special gift from someone?

11. Some very important people reappear in Jillian and John's lives. Some, like Marty and Carol, are real blessings. Others, like Monica and Dr. Jeffrey A. Lawrence, are real challenges. Have you ever had someone pop back into your life? What were the blessings and challenges you faced?

12. Even though Nancy loves Buck, she is still hanging on to the vestiges of her past, trying to be faithful to the memory of her late husband, the father of her children. Have you, or someone you know, ever been in a similar situation? How did you/she/he work things out?

13. Jillian predicts that things will not go well with Monica on the movie set, especially away from home territory in Alaska, yet

she lets things take their course (at least at the beginning.) What would have been your response/plan in such a situation?

14. Chase Cheekwood is used to having any woman he wants. Have you ever met someone like him (male or female?) What do you think about the way Jillian handled his advances?

15. Several new families are created in this book—Pete, Kelly, and the twins; Karen, Robert, and Rick; John, Jillian, Marty, and the extended Romano family; Carol, Jerry, Alan, and Bev. Their lives drastically change in the period of a year or less. Share a similar experience of your own.

16. John wishes he could have done things differently when it came to his relationship with his late brother, Anthony. Do you think it is possible to make things better—even when someone is no longer living?

17. Things are going very well for Maria in her new business. Sometimes, however, there are downsides to "success," not only in her case, but for John in his acting and Jillian with her book. Discuss them, and the possible ways to deal with them. Do you think the positives outweigh the negatives?

18. John realizes his dream achievement, and then finds there are much more important things in his life than winning an Academy Award. Have you ever made a similar discovery?

19. John and Jillian happily celebrate their first anniversary with family and friends, and give each other the "gift" of the Esperanza Workshop, a project to help others outside of their family. They feel it was the perfect anniversary. What would be your perfect way to celebrate a special milestone in your own life?

20. Who do you think made the anonymous million-dollar donation to the Esperanza Workshop? Why?

Check out the entire NOTED! series.

Kathy J. Jacobson

Author's Note/Acknowledgments

A reader of *On Another Note (Noted! Book 2)* recently thanked me for taking her to places she will never be able to travel. She also wondered if I wasn't getting the chance to relive some of the amazing travel experiences I've been blessed with over the years by writing them into my story. I would venture to say there is some truth in her assumption.

But travel is not the only experience that has shaped my life and my stories. After graduating from the University of Wisconsin with a degree in sociology, I embarked on a ten-year-long career working in the juvenile justice system. Over those years, I met thousands of young people, many of them neglected or abused in various ways like "Rick." I also met some wonderful couples who opened their hearts and their homes to some of the more fortunate youths and changed their lives forever. Writing *A New Note* has helped me remember some of that hopefulness, and I pray that it passes on to all those who are in need of it today.

A huge thank you to my family—husband, Jeff; daughter, Kirsten; son, Spencer, and his wife, Emily; son, Jens; my cousins, Judy and Pam; the Jacobson clan; and my hospice and church families for their ongoing love and support. A special thanks to Cleo Ware for reading the manuscript. I couldn't do this without all of you!

About the Author

Kathy J. Jacobson has worked in various forms of ministry over the past twenty years—from youth and Christian education coordinator to campus ministry and rural parish ministry to hospice chaplain.

She lives in the beautiful "Driftless Area" of Southwestern Wisconsin with her husband, Jeff. They have three "children"—all "twenty-something." She is an avid traveler, with most memorable trips to the Holy Land, Papua New Guinea, and Tanzania. She loves music, the theater, and sports, but her true passion is writing. A *New Note* is the third book in the *Noted!* "faithful fiction" series.